D0628220

SPECIAL MESSAGE TO READERS

THE ULVERSCROFT FOUNDATION
(registered UK charity number 264873)

was established in 1972 to provide funds for research, diagnosis and treatment of eye diseases. Examples of major projects funded by the Ulverscroft Foundation are:-

- The Children's Eye Unit at Moorfields Eye Hospital, London
- The Ulverscroft Children's Eye Unit at Great Ormond Street Hospital for Sick Children
- Funding research into eye diseases and treatment at the Department of Ophthalmology, University of Leicester
- The Ulverscroft Vision Research Group, Institute of Child Health
- Twin operating theatres at the Western Ophthalmic Hospital, London
- The Chair of Ophthalmology at the Royal Australian College of Ophthalmologists

You can help further the work of the Foundation by making a donation or leaving a legacy. Every contribution is gratefully received. If you would like to help support the Foundation or require further information, please contact:

THE ULVERSCROFT FOUNDATION
The Green, Bradgate Road, Anstey
Leicester LE7 7FU, England
Tel: (0116) 236 4325

website: www.foundation.ulverscroft.com

RUBY LOVES . . .

Crime writer Adam finds the peace he needs to finish his latest novel in a remote stately home in Carwyn Bay, Wales — at least until effervescent, disaster-prone Ruby arrives to run the tourist café while also pursuing a secret plan to uncover her grandfather's past. Through baking disasters and shocking revelations, they find themselves falling in love. But Ruby is saddened by what she learns about her grandfather, and plans to go home to America at the end of the summer. Will their relationship be strong enough to last?

Books by Christina Garbutt
in the Linford Romance Library:

MYSTERY AT MORWENNA BAY
THE LOCKET OF LOGAN HALL

CHRISTINA GARBUTT

RUBY LOVES . . .

Complete and Unabridged

LINFORD
Leicester

First published in Great Britain in 2018

First Linford Edition
published 2020

A catalogue record for this book is available
from the British Library.

ISBN 978–1–4448–4358–3

Published by
F. A. Thorpe (Publishing)
Anstey, Leicestershire

Set by Words & Graphics Ltd.
Anstey, Leicestershire
Printed and bound in Great Britain by
T. J. International Ltd., Padstow, Cornwall

This book is printed on acid-free paper

1

The girl was back on the beach again, a splash of bright colour against the pale sand. He'd seen her there for three days in a row.

She was easy to spot with her brightly coloured outfits fluttering in the brisk, spring breeze. She'd scrambled over rocks, peered into caves and eaten picnics while watching the waves.

Yesterday had been different. She'd been wearing a red hat and an equally red dress and she'd sat on an exposed rock and gazed at Melveryn Manor, the house in which he was staying, for half an hour. Adam, unseen, had watched her back, intrigued despite himself.

Today she was marching purposefully across the sand towards the house, her footprints cutting a direct line through the newly uncovered sand. Wild hair was flying everywhere as she strode and her bright yellow dress pushed against her legs one minute and billowed out the next.

Adam sighed, disappointed. If she thought he was going to come out and give her an interview or an autograph she was very much mistaken. No one was supposed to know he was staying at the manor but someone from the village had obviously blabbed.

It had to be Estelle; no one else knew he was here. Never mind, if she knocked at the door he would ignore it. He was almost master level at ignoring things that didn't interest him; at least that's what his ex-fiancée claimed.

He turned his attention back to his screen. He managed two lines before his attention was broken again by persistent knocking.

He ignored it. The girl would get bored and go away eventually. Tomorrow he'd go down to the village and have a word with Estelle, who managed the house and who'd rented him the suite of rooms. He'd taken them for some peaceful privacy and he'd believed her when she'd said she'd keep his presence quiet.

It seemed his trust had been broken, which was annoying but inevitable. Everyone loved to gossip and eventually gave in to temptation.

He was frustrated, though; he didn't want to move again after he'd spent so long looking for a place like this. His little part of the house, as far away as it was from any other houses and with its sweeping views and comfortable rooms, was perfect for him.

He understood from Estelle that the rest of the house was opened to the public at the weekends during the summer months. A small number of tourists liked to wander through the rooms in which the Renaissance author Maurice Henry had written his celebrated masterpiece. He'd been assured they wouldn't be able to access Adam's suite and he had a private front door so he could come and go as he pleased.

It had sounded exactly what he

required — but if there were already rumours of his presence then he would terminate his lease and find somewhere else. He didn't want to be disturbed at all.

Eventually the knocking stopped and he immersed himself once more in the world he was creating on screen. An hour passed, and his left shoulder started to complain at the length of time he'd been sitting in the same position.

He stood and stretched. Since he'd turned forty he'd found he couldn't sit for long periods at the computer any more. He needed a walk.

The weather was mild for the middle of May but he tugged on a jumper. The sea breeze could be very cooling and sometimes a T-shirt wasn't enough. He patted his jeans to make sure he had his keys and his phone and, reassured by the familiar lumps, he pulled open the front door.

He stepped outside — or, at least, he tried to. Something was blocking his way and he tripped.

Trying to right himself, he managed a few ungainly steps into the garden before his legs gave way and he landed on his knees in an overgrown flower-bed.

'Oh my goodness,' said a voice from behind him. 'Are you all right? No, that's a silly question — of course you're not. You're in a flowerbed when you wanted to be standing. Here — let me help.'

A slim arm slid underneath his and he caught a glimpse of sunshine yellow. Then he was being lightly but ineffectively tugged.

'I'm fine,' he said sharply, pulling his arm free and pushing himself upright.

He swung round to face the voice, unsurprised to see the girl from the beach on his doorstep.

She was taller than he'd guessed from afar, not a great deal shorter than his six foot, although her head of very tight, brown curls might have added an inch or two. Her skin was pale with a slight smattering of freckles over her nose, and in her left hand she held a brightly coloured hat. Her accent suggested she was from the States, probably the east. Her hazel eyes were filled with concern and he felt like a prat for falling.

'I'm so sorry,' she said. 'I thought you were out so I was waiting for you. I was expecting you to come from the other direction.'

She gestured behind him towards the steep path, which led down to the beach and which was meant to be private and only accessible to him. Surely she'd seen all the *Keep Out* signs. They were hardly welcoming.

'Look,' he said, as angry at being humiliated in front of a pretty girl as he was about his peace being destroyed, 'I don't know what Estelle has told you — '

'Oh, not much,' she said, smiling. 'Just that you'd be able to let me in until they can get me a key cut. She said you'd probably be in this morning so I thought I would call round, and when you weren't here I decided to wait. It's a beautiful view. I'm going to love seeing it all the time.'

'What?' he said, alarmed.

Fans sometimes did get a little obsessive but he'd never had one think she was moving in with him before. He was dealing with a mad woman. How long would it take for the police to get over here? He glanced down towards the little town nestled next to the bay, a good ten minutes' walk away, and without a police station of its own. It would take them a while. He'd have to be firm and get rid of her by himself.

'You've wasted your time,' he said sternly. 'You'll need to return to the village — and not come back.'

It finally seemed to register on her face that he wasn't being friendly. The light dimmed in her eyes and a small crease of concern formed on the bridge of her nose.

'But Estelle said you could let me through. I promise I won't take up any more of your time.'

'Let you through?'

'Into the main house. I know it doesn't officially open to the public for another couple of weeks but I wanted to get a head start on everything that needs doing. I don't think anyone's dusted in there since the rooms closed to the public last year. Can you imagine the cobwebs?' She shuddered.

Adam rubbed his hand over his face. This conversation was getting away from him.

'Let's start again,' he said wearily. 'Why are you here?'

'Oh, yes. I should have mentioned that first. I got distracted when you fell. Estelle's employed me to look after the house when it opens. I'm going to be taking money from the guests and making them tea and doing things like that.'

'Oh,' he said, 'right, well . . . ' He cleared his throat and ran a hand through his hair. He could feel blood rushing to his face. He hoped he didn't look as red as he felt. In his arrogance he'd made a fool of himself — but at least he knew that Estelle hadn't betrayed him after all.

He started again in what he hoped was a friendlier voice, 'You're absolutely right, I can let you into the main building. Please come through.'

She beamed at him and he winced. She was like a burst of sunshine in his grey existence.

Together they stepped into the quiet of the house. The dark wood panelling provided a sudden contrast to the bright outdoors. He led her down the narrow corridor which separated his rooms from the others. Her shoes slapped loudly on the wooden floor behind him. Not a girl overly given to quietness, he guessed.

'Have you been staying here long?' she asked.

'A while,' he said.

'It's such a beautiful place. I can't wait to get settled.'

'What?' he said again, swinging round to face her. She careened into him and he caught a whiff of floral perfume before she leaped back.

'Sorry,' she said. 'I'm so clumsy. Grams always says I should wear padding.'

'What do you mean about getting settled?' he asked, ignoring her comment about Grams, whoever that was. The word 'settled' sounded more permanent than coming in at the weekends to do a bit of tea making.

'I'm going to be staying in the main house,' she said, beaming at him as if she was sharing the best news. 'There's a room and a kitchenette for the person who looks after the house. It's tiny apparently but it's rent-free, which is great because I'm going to be over here for another three months and I was worried about paying for accommodation all that time. I'm an assistant professor in Stanmore University in Pennsylvania. I teach English Literature with a background in mythology. I'm having a little sabbatical to research Celtic mythology in a true Celtic setting. It's not like I can do that at home, is it? To be able to stay in the great Maurice Henry's house while I'm doing the research is a dream come true!'

Had she even stopped for breath during that monologue?

'You don't need to worry about me, though,' she carried on. 'Estelle told me you're very busy working away although she was very hush-hush about what you do, so obviously I'm very intrigued. But I won't pry. As soon as I've had my key cut I won't bother you. You won't even know I'm here.'

He seriously doubted that.

'Shall we — ' She gestured behind him, indicating the door behind him that led into the main house. He shook his head resignedly.

'Of course,' he said.

He unlocked the door and stepped to one side so she could pass. The sweet smell of her perfume hit him once again as she sailed past him into the grand hallway of Maurice Henry's house. Such was her enthusiasm, she almost bounced into the centre of the room before stopping.

'Wow,' she said, spinning in a circle and gazing up in wonder.

Adam had felt just like that when he'd stepped into the house for the first time. Although not large for a stately home, Melveryn Manor was beautifully proportioned. They were standing in a large square hallway with a sweeping staircase leading upwards to a wide landing. Doors headed off in every direction and large windows lined the front of the house so anyone standing inside had uninterrupted views of the panoramic coastline.

'Can I leave you now?' he asked, his words sounding harsher than he'd intended.

'Of course,' she said, her good humour undimmed by his surliness. 'I didn't introduce myself before and as we're going to be roommates, I really feel I should. I'm Ruby Turner.'

She held out a hand and he took it, his big hand swallowing her dainty one.

'I'm Adam Jacobs.'

12

'Oh, like that gruesome author? I bet you get that a lot. Have you read anything by him? I had to read his first one, *Open Nights*, I think it's called, for an undergraduate class I took years ago. The story was horrible. Full of blood and gore. Grams loves his stuff but then she loves a grisly novel. I can't stand that sort of thing myself. Adam Jacobs must have a real twisted mind. I mean, who thinks of murder all the time?'

She gave a theatrical shudder and Adam felt the corners of his mouth tug. It was such a long time since he'd smiled properly that he almost didn't recognise the sensation.

'So what is it that you do, Mr Jacobs?' she asked, even though a few minutes ago she'd promised not to pry. Adam felt his stomach quiver with suppressed laughter.

'I write about fictional, gruesome murders, Ms Turner. And my first novel was called *Closed Nights*, not Open, although I think your version sounds better. I wish I'd thought of it.'

And then he did smile, a proper full smile, which started in his stomach and made his face ache, because it turned out he'd finally said something to quieten the motor-mouth.

She was standing stock still in the centre of the hallway, her mouth open like an oversized fish.

'Let me know when you wish to leave,' he said, enjoying her discomfort perhaps more than was polite. 'In the meantime, would you prefer me to lock the door between us?'

She didn't answer. He winked and then pulled the connecting door closed.

2

Ruby talked too much when she was nervous. She knew she did. She tried really hard to stop the habit. As she'd grown older she almost always succeeded but today she'd messed up.

But then who could blame her? It wasn't every day that a handsome man literally fell at her feet and, because she'd been the cause of his face-plant into the rampant weeds, she had gone into embarrassed overdrive. The whole meeting had been a disaster from start to finish.

Even when he'd fallen in an untidy heap at her feet she could tell Adam was a good-looking man. He had broad shoulders, long legs and an athletic physique. When he'd stood up and turned round to look at her, her stomach had fluttered oddly.

He was taller than her, which with

her height was unusual. His dark hair was greying at the temples and even the fact that he was annoyed and embarrassed didn't detract from his startlingly dark blue eyes. It didn't matter that she thought he was the most attractive man she'd seen in a long time, because everything that had happened during their entire meeting had been an embarrassing shambles. He probably thought she was an idiot.

She'd tripped him into a flower bed and then insulted him so badly it was a wonder he hadn't stormed off. She'd practically called him a psychopath. When she told Mom and Grams they'd laugh so hard, they'd cry. Maybe she wouldn't mention the whole episode when she Skyped them later; it might undermine how well she was doing with every other part of her plan.

She sighed. It was time to forget about Adam Jacobs and focus on the job in hand.

She rummaged around in her handbag and pulled out the floor plan

Estelle had given her earlier. It marked out which rooms were going to be open to the public and which ones were hers for the summer. She decided to look at her own first. Looking around the rest of the house would be a treat to save for later.

She headed round to the back of the staircase where she found a door that was plain in comparison to the other more ornate woodwork dotted around the hallway. This was clearly the servants' passageway through the house. She pushed open the door and stepped through into a narrow corridor.

She still couldn't believe her luck as she followed the hallway leading away from the front door towards the back of the house and down some steep stone steps. She'd been puzzling over how she was going to get time to wander, unsupervised, around Melveryn Manor and then the solution had fallen into her lap.

She'd been in a local café eating the most wonderful toffee cake when she'd spotted a postcard wedged under one of the table legs. It had obviously fallen down from a small display in the window. She'd pulled the card out, meaning to stick it back up, and then she'd noticed that written on it, in neat penmanship, was an advertisement for a summer job.

The person responsible for the advert was looking for someone to man the entrance to Melveryn Manor and at the same time run a small café every weekend during the summer months. The applicant needed to be familiar with Maurice Henry and be able to bake. The pay was pitiful but the applicant would be able to stay rent-free — and, most importantly, unsupervised — at Melveryn Manor.

Ruby had all but sprinted back to the guest house she was staying at with the postcard tucked securely in her hand-bag. Once in the safety of her room she'd called the number on the card and had been given an interview within the hour. It was lucky that she'd taught a module on Maurice Henry last semester because she'd been able to talk about him with confidence, so much so that the interview had skimmed over her ability to bake; which was just as well because she couldn't. But how hard could it be? All she had to do was stick a few ingredients in a cake tin and throw the mixture in the oven.

She ran down the last of the steps and came to a large room with a bed in one corner, a couple of threadbare sofas and a small kitchenette in the far corner. It was a bit sparse, but with a cheerful rug thrown down and some flowers for the little dining table, the room would be brighter and more homely. It didn't really matter what it was like; it was functional and she wasn't planning on spending a lot of time in this room anyway. She would be able to explore the Manor to her heart's content and that was all that mattered.

There were two other doors in the room she was in. One led Ruby into a miniscule but thankfully clean bathroom and the other led up another flight of stone steps.

'At least I'll be fit after this summer,' Ruby muttered to herself as she made her way up the steps to a new section of the house.

This time she emerged into a pristine, modern kitchen. Estelle had told her that cleaners had come in and made sure the room was up to hygiene standards so it was ready for her to prepare food. She grimaced at the thought, then pushed the worry aside. There were two weeks until the house opened; that was plenty of time to learn to make basic dishes. She was an intelligent woman with two degrees to her name. She could learn how to put a decent sandwich together.

Through an open door, she could see what looked like seating for the café. She stepped through and found a room with five sets of chairs and tables. The tables were decorated in red-checked tablecloths and plastic flowers. By the side of the ancient till was a price list for entrance into the Manor. Customers had to come through the café entrance to access the house.

It was a shame they wouldn't be able to enter through the grand front doors but Ruby couldn't be in two places at once and she understood that there was only enough money in the Maurice Henry trust fund to pay for one member of staff.

She wandered over to a table and picked up a menu. As she read through it, her heart sank.

'Oh man,' she said to herself when she'd come to the end of the list. 'I have absolutely no idea what half of these things even are. I mean, what an earth is brown sauce?'

'It's a condiment that tastes particularly good with bacon,' said a deep voice from behind her.

Ruby screamed and clutched at her chest. Her heart was trying to escape from her rib cage.

'I didn't mean to scare you,' said the

voice, clearly very amused. 'I've got to go out now and so I need to lock up.'

Ruby turned to see Adam standing behind her, his blue eyes full of laughter.

'I think you've given me a heart attack,' she accused him breathlessly.

'Sorry,' he said, not sounding at all apologetic.

He stood watching her. He was even handsomer now that he was amused and not annoyed.

'Can we go?' he asked, nodding towards the open door.

'Sure,' she said, popping the menu into her handbag. She'd need to go through it later with the benefit of an internet connection. She knew the British ate weird things but *Spotted Dick* sounded gruesome. She dreaded to think what the ingredients might be.

'How did you find me?' she asked as they made their way back down the stairs to her new living space.

'I just followed the trail of open doors,' he said.

'Oh,' she said, unsure what to reply. He'd said it mildly but his words sounded like a criticism.

'This isn't lovely, is it?' he commented as they stepped into her new living space.

'It only needs a little bit of brightening up,' she said cheerfully.

'It needs ripping out and starting again.'

'It's not that bad, it's . . . ' She stopped. She was going to learn to be quiet even when nervous. It really didn't matter what he thought of the room, he wasn't going to be living in it. The more she talked, the more likely she was to put her foot in it again.

He didn't press her to carry on and once he'd swept his eyes critically over the room and its tatty furniture, he turned and made his way back up the stairs into the main body of the house.

She followed him, trying not to pant. Hopefully she'd discover a quicker route through the house over the next few days; preferably a route with a lot less stairs. Although she did get to admire Adam's physique as he powered ahead of her.

He whisked her through his part of the house without stopping. Soon they were on his doorstep with him firmly locking the door behind them.

'I rang Estelle,' he said. 'She's had a key cut for you this afternoon so you can access your side of the house from tomorrow. You won't need to come this way again.'

Ruby could take a hint. He wanted to be left alone. Fine; so did she. Solitude would give her plenty of time to conduct her research.

'Also,' he continued, 'I'd be grateful if you didn't let anyone know I was here. I find it very distracting when people call round expecting me to discuss my novels or to give them autographs or something. I'm trying to finish my latest novel and it's proving harder work than normal.'

'I can't tell anyone?' she queried.

'I suppose you *can* tell everyone

— but I'd be grateful if you didn't,' he clarified.

'Well that's something of a relief I must say. I wasn't looking forward to telling Grams I'd insulted one of her favourite authors but I normally tell her everything. If I'm forbidden from mentioning anything about you, then I can avoid telling her altogether. I mean . . . '

Ruby slammed her mouth closed. She was doing it again; rambling. It was just that he was piercing her with that bright blue gaze and she found it unsettling.

They stood for a moment.

'Right, well, I'll head off,' she said when she couldn't bear the silence any longer.

'OK, I guess I'll see you around.'

She nodded and set off down the path to the beach, leaving him standing on his front step. She felt his gaze on her back long after she'd left. It was weird that he hadn't moved or come with her. This path was the only way in and out of the garden and so he must be waiting for her to go before he went wherever he was going. He obviously didn't want to make polite conversation with her on the way down to the beach. What strange people the British were!

* * *

Her room back at the guest house was welcoming. She'd only been staying for five days but the place already felt like home with its little desk for writing and deliciously comfortable window seat, where she could sit and watch as people wandered the high street. She sank gratefully onto the soft mattress of her bed and inhaled the fresh linen smell. She'd miss someone cleaning for her when she was living on her own again.

She rummaged in her handbag and pulled out her phone and the menu. She needed to look up what each dish required, then work out a way of creating them with ease. Once that was out of the way, she could concentrate on her real mission.

Without a printer she had to make notes on what she found by hand and she'd covered ten sheets of A4 paper in increasingly erratic handwriting before she gave up. She'd go and see Estelle and find out if she really had to make all these cakes from scratch. Surely there was a wholesaler who could provide this sort of thing?

Estelle's estate agency was a few doors down from the guest house on the main high street. She slipped on her favourite pair of flats and made her way across the cobblestones. Peering in through the agency window, she saw Estelle sitting at her computer, her glasses resting in her greying, back-combed hair.

'Hello,' she cried when she caught sight of Ruby hovering at the window. 'Do come in. How was your morning? Did you make a good start?'

'I only had time for a quick look about before Mr Jacobs had to leave and so he needed to lock up,' said Ruby, coming into the office and plonking herself on a chair near Estelle's desk.

'Of course. It was silly of me not to check we still had spare keys before today. I've got a new set for you here.'

Estelle rummaged through the stacks of paperwork covering her desk before pulling out a bunch of keys.

'Here you go, darling. I'm afraid they're not labelled but I'm sure you'll figure out which one fits where easily.'

'Thanks,' said Ruby, pocketing the keys. 'I had a look at the menu while I was up at the manor and . . . '

'Oh, that's good of you,' said Estelle. 'You are organised. As you can see there's nothing fancy on the menu. I did think that you could have a specials board if you like. You could add some good American home cooking to that.'

'Um, well, yes,' said Ruby. That was never going to happen. Ruby didn't bake American cakes any better than British ones but Estelle didn't need to know that. 'It's just that I'm unfamiliar with some of the terms on the list. I was wondering if I could make some changes — '

'Oh no, I don't think so,' said Estelle, all her wrinkles turning downwards in concern. 'Melveryn Manor guests are very traditional. They love a good home-made cake. It's why a lot of them go to the manor. Most of the locals know all there is to know about Maurice Henry and don't even bother to look around the house any more.'

'Really?' queried Ruby, feeling out of her depth and wishing she hadn't been quite so gung-ho about applying for the catering job.

'Oh yes,' said Estelle, gathering a handful of the beads around her neck and running them through her fingers. 'Captain's Cabin at the end of the high street will have some traditional British cookery books. I can let you have some money out of the kitty to buy one. I'm sure when you've had a read through you'll find an American equivalent for most things. If you've experience of baking, you'll pick the recipes up quickly.'

Ruby nodded miserably and waited

while Estelle disappeared into a back room, her jewellery jangling, then handed over several notes.

'Thank you,' said Ruby.

'Pop back in a few days and let me know how you're getting on.'

'Sure,' said Ruby, but Estelle wasn't looking at her any more. She'd resumed typing, the tip of her tongue poking out as she concentrated.

Ruby let herself out and wandered disconsolately down the busy street. Her trip to Wales been going so well. She didn't want a little thing like not being able to cook to get in her way.

She'd loved Carwyn Bay from the moment she'd arrived. With its narrow, winding street full of different shops and its walkway covered in bumpy cobblestones, the small town was pretty much what she'd imagined a British street would look like. The shops were mostly independents and she loved poking around in their treasure troves. Yesterday she'd found a beret which matched her favourite yellow dress

— and which she'd now realised she'd left at Melveryn Manor when she'd visited earlier.

Today she made it to Captain's Cabin without noticing her surroundings. She was beginning to think she'd bitten off way more than she could chew. Yes, Melveryn Manor meant a lot to her family — but could she pay the price when she let Estelle and all the regular customers down so spectacularly? She needed to focus.

She'd been in Captain's Cabin a few times. It was an odd shop. It sold brightly coloured buckets and spades, beach balls and windmills. You could get virtually any ice-cream you wanted — but at the back, covered in dust, were random things. Ruby had found a carriage clock and a deerstalker hat a few days ago.

Today she headed over to the book section.

'Can I help you, dear?' asked an older lady in a peacock-blue dress that Ruby envied. The lady was standing behind the till and watching Ruby with undisguised interest.

'I'm looking for a traditional cookery book,' said Ruby. 'With really simple instructions.'

'I know just the thing,' said the lady as she stepped out from behind the counter. 'Are you from America, dear?' she asked as she rummaged through the books, which were stacked in no discernable order.

'Yes, I'm over for the summer. I'm researching Celtic mythology but I'm also going to work at Melveryn Manor.'

'Oh, how lovely. I'm Jo and I do enjoy going up there during the summer and taking tea in the gardens with my friends. The view from the terrace is breathtaking.'

'Ah,' said Ruby. 'I'll be seeing you there then.'

'Here you go,' declared Jo, pulling out a large cookbook. 'This will give you a very basic introduction to cooking some of our British favourites. I imagine it's quite different from what you're used to.'

'Indeed,' said Ruby, taking the book and flicking through the pages. The contents did seem very comprehensive. Her spirits started to rise again. It wouldn't be so difficult after all.

'You might also like this,' suggested Jo. 'It's a visual history of Melveryn Manor.'

'Thank you,' said Ruby eagerly, putting the cookery book down and flicking through the picture book.

She was nearing the end when she saw him. It was a grainy, black and white picture and in it he was younger than she'd ever seen him before.

She ran a finger lightly across his face. His smile had never changed. He'd worn it every day until he died. Whenever she thought of him, that was how she pictured him; sitting in Grams' kitchen wearing that smile.

'Oh, Pops,' she murmured as she closed the book gently. It was her first clue into the mystery no one in her family understood. Why had her beloved grandfather run away from home at twenty-two and never come back? He'd never even mentioned the town where he'd grown up, until his confused last days when he'd thought he'd been back in Melveryn Manor . . . and he'd not been happy about it. Not at all!

3

Adam leaned back in his chair and sniffed. Was something burning? Again? He got up from his desk and made his way to the door connecting his suite with the rest of Melveryn Manor.

The smell of was stronger here. Adam hadn't seen Ruby since she'd moved into her apartment ten days ago but he had smelled burning on more than one occasion. What on earth was she doing in there?

A shrill noise split the air and Adam groaned. Whatever Ruby was doing had set the fire alarm off. He took a step back towards his office; it was none of his business.

The noise carried on. It would be quicker to go and reset the alarm himself. It would certainly be quieter. And he couldn't deny that he was curious.

True to her word, Ruby had not come to see him since she'd moved into her side of the manor house. He was surprised. He'd imagined that she was a girl who loved company and conversation, but she'd not bothered him and there'd been no visitors to see her. He'd heard her a few times, moving heavy items about and singing to herself in a clear, lyrical voice that was beautiful rather than annoying.

The fire alarm had been ringing for over a minute and there was no sign of it stopping. Decision made, Adam let himself into the main house and made his way to the café.

He found Ruby standing in front of an ancient control panel, her face bright red as she pressed fruitlessly at buttons. She didn't seem to notice his approach but she didn't flinch when he leaned over her and pulled a large red lever. The noise stopped abruptly.

'Thank you.' She breathed out, fanning her face ineffectively with her hand. 'What a nightmare!'

He took a step away from her and asked, 'Is anything on fire?'

'No . . . well . . . not exactly.' Ruby shifted on her feet and refused to meet his eye.

He grinned. It was the first time he'd smiled since he'd last seen her. She seemed to have that effect on him and he wasn't sure if he liked it. He was straight-faced by the time she flicked her eyes towards him — although it was a struggle when he took in her face, covered in dust and sweat and still red, either with effort or embarrassment. She turned her eyes away.

'What was on fire?' he asked.

'Um . . . ' She tilted her head and looked past him into the kitchen. She clearly did not want to tell him. He waited patiently.

Eventually she said, 'I was in another part of the house and I hadn't realised time had passed so quickly. Some muffins were in the oven and they didn't so much catch fire as smoked. A lot.'

How long did it take muffins to start smoking? How long could she possibly have left them? An hour, maybe. Who got so carried away with cleaning they forgot about something they were cooking — and why was she cooking muffins anyway? The house didn't open up for another week. She was very puzzling.

'Do you need a hand cleaning up the kitchen?' he asked politely.

He didn't know why he'd offered. He was at a critical point in his novel. His murderer was about to strike and he normally hated to stop work when he reached a pivotal moment. But his concentration was broken anyway and she was amusing. He hadn't seen another person for several days, which was probably the reason he was keen to hang around. He should get out more.

'No, it's fine, thank you,' she said, still not meeting his eyes.

He was intrigued.

'I insist.' He started to make his way over to the kitchen but she darted in front of him.

'I wouldn't want to interrupt your day. I'm sure you're very busy.'

'Not too busy to help a neighbour,' he said, skirting round her.

He was being an interfering busybody and he was loving it. What could be so bad that she was hurrying in front of him and blocking his entrance to the kitchen?

'I insist that you don't come in,' she said, her eyes wild with panic.

'If you don't let me in then you leave me with no choice but to contact Estelle and tell her that something strange is going on.'

He'd do no such thing but she didn't know that.

She sagged and hung her head miserably.

'OK,' she said, 'but you'll probably go to Estelle anyway when you've seen what I've done.'

She stood aside to let him pass. He stopped on the threshold. The room was a disaster zone. Every surface was covered in baking paraphernalia with blobs of goo splattered here and there. Splats of flour coated most of the floor.

'What . . . ?' he started.

Ruby shuffled into the kitchen behind him.

'I . . . ' he said. 'You . . . '

'I can't bake,' she stated.

'Oh,' he said.

'I can't cook very well either.'

'I see,' he said, his stomach muscles quivering with suppressed laughter.

'I'm trying. I thought baking would be an easy skill to pick up, but . . . '

He snorted and tried to cover it up with a cough.

'I can cook,' he said, 'and I'm not bad at baking either.'

'Good for you,' she said sarcastically.

'I can show you how,' he clarified.

'Why would you do that?' she asked.

Good question. Helping her would take time; a lot of it if the look of her previous attempts was anything to go by.

'In exchange for my help, you're going to tell me why you're really here.'

She walked over to the smouldering tray of muffins and dumped the offending cakes into the bin. They made a hefty thump as they hit whatever they landed on. Probably an equally solid cake!

'I told you why I'm here,' she said, as she pulled a sweeping brush out of a cupboard and began to tackle the piles of flour. 'I'm researching Celtic mythology. I wanted to be in Wales, where so many of the stories have been passed down into local legend.'

He didn't tell her that he'd looked her up after their first meeting. He'd found that she was well-known and respected in her field with lots of papers accredited to her name. He'd read a few that were available online and he was impressed. She wrote concisely and clearly, never patronising the reader or overwhelming them with overly complicated jargon. She had a first class degree in Literature and a PhD in Ancient Mythology so that part of her story was true — but what was a scholar doing working for a pittance as a baker, especially when that scholar couldn't bake?

'I've no doubt you're researching mythology,' he said. 'But that's not the reason you're staying and working at Melveryn Manor. You can't possibly need the money and if you can't bake, why would you apply to run a café? There has to be more to your story than you're letting on.'

As he spoke she collected the used dishes and started placing them in the large stainless steel sink, keeping her back turned to him at all times. She turned the tap on and he waited.

When the sink was full, she said, 'I haven't lied to anyone.'

'I never said you had. I just think there's more to the story than you're letting on. I'm not planning on telling anyone if that's what you're worried about. I enjoy a good story.'

She sighed, 'Fine. I'll tell you in exchange for several cookery lessons.'

'Great,' he said, although he'd decide

at the end of this session whether he'd come back or not. 'Wash up that mixing bowl and the sieve while I find some cake tins, and we'll get started.'

By the time she'd washed and dried the two cooking utensils he'd found the ingredients he wanted and had laid them out on the kitchen table. It had taken him a while to clean the work surface — some cake mixture from a previous baking calamity had bonded almost permanently with its top — but after some vigorous rubbing it had cleaned up well.

'We'll start with a basic Victoria sponge. It's a traditional British classic as well as being easy to make,' he said.

'It's *not* easy to make,' insisted Ruby, pushing herself away from the counter she was leaning against and opening the fridge door. 'This is the most successful one I've made.'

She held out an almost flat disc wrapped in cling film, the sponge so hard it remained rigid even as the cake dangled from her fingers.

'It tastes OK,' she said defensively.

And that did it. He couldn't contain the laughter. Before he knew it he was doubled up and wheezing. After a few minutes of battling to get himself under control he straightened to look at her. He was shocked to see tears running down her face but then he realised she was laughing as well and that set him off again.

'Wow,' he said when they finally had themselves under control. 'You truly cannot bake.'

'Yes, and I will be eternally grateful if you can teach me. How did you learn?'

'My mother taught me,' he said.

He could still feel how it felt to be perched on a chair next to her, his fingers sticky with dough as they sieved and folded together. He could hear her warm laugh and the rustle of her apron against the work surface. He felt a rush of love for his mum, followed by a wave of guilt when he thought how long it had been since he'd seen her.

His parents lived near London so

popping in for a quick visit wasn't possible, but that was a flimsy excuse. With no set working hours he could easily visit them for a long weekend if he really wanted to. He'd shut himself off from the world, but he shouldn't have shut his parents out as well. He'd ring his mum this evening and perhaps arrange a visit.

'It's basic because there are so few ingredients; it's only sugar, eggs, butter and self-raising flour. Once you've mastered this you should be able to move on to more complicated cakes.'

She groaned and rested her head in her hands.

'I will never master it,' she said. 'I'm one of those people who can't cook.'

'Everyone can cook. Come on, I'll show you.'

She pulled a recipe book off a shelf.

'I'll make notes, while you talk,' she said.

He nodded. It was what he would do in the same situation. He talked her through each step, explaining that the mixture needed lots of air otherwise the cake would end up flat once baked, pointing out — almost without laughing — that this may have been where she'd gone wrong before. When they'd put two cake tins in the oven he showed her how to whip up some buttercream icing, which was his preferred filling in a Victoria sponge. She insisted he sit down while she cleaned up, and made him a cup of tea. The tea was exactly how he liked it and he told her so.

'If all else fails, at least I know I can make a decent cup of tea,' she said.

She chatted at him as she washed dishes. She could talk about everything and nothing and her hands whizzed everywhere as she spoke. She must be a mesmerising lecturer.

She was evidently hoping he'd forgotten his demand to get her to reveal why she was here. He smiled as she talked about finding dust bunnies the size of rats in some of the rooms she'd cleaned, then segued into her opinion as to whether the Thor legend was well represented in the Marvel films about the Norse god.

She could try to distract him but he wasn't leaving until he found out what was going on. It wasn't a hardship to watch an attractive young woman chatter away while he waited.

When the timer pinged up he triumphantly pulled two golden, circular cakes out of the oven.

'Wow,' she said reverently. 'They look amazing.'

'Press gently here,' he said, pointing to the middle of the cake.

He watched as a long, slender finger very delicately touched the sponge. The cake indented slightly and sprang back up.

'If the cake hadn't come back up like that then you'd need to put it back in the oven for a few minutes. If the sponge felt solid, then chances are you'd need to start again.'

She nodded solemnly.

'Normally I'd suggest we leave them to cool for a bit before doing the filling but I'm in a hurry.'

He watched as she spread the buttercream on one half and a layer of strawberry jam on the other with the concentration of a neurosurgeon.

'Shall we try a piece?' she asked once the two halves of the cake were sandwiched together, the buttercream melting slightly on the warm sponge.

'Yeah, we can do that while you tell me about yourself.'

She groaned.

'Do I have to?' she asked.

'Yes.'

'It's not really my story to tell,' she tried.

He wasn't going to be put off. He'd already taken two hours out of his writing day. She owed him.

'You've not told anyone I'm here. I won't tell anyone your story,' he promised.

'OK,' she said resignedly. 'Let's take the cake through to the café and I'll tell you all about it.'

She cut them both generous slices

and his stomach growled. He realised he'd missed lunch and it was nearing dinner time.

She handed him a fork. He took it and followed her into the café. They each took a seat near one of the windows.

'I could never tire of that view,' she said as she gazed out at the rugged cliffs.

Whereas his suite of rooms looked out over the beach, the café's windows looked out over a long stretch of coastline. In front of them now the headland was visible for miles in each direction and the silvery, rolling mass of the sea stretched out as far as the eye could see.

'It's stunning,' he agreed, 'but don't try and distract me. What's your story?'

She took a big forkful of cake.

'Oh my goodness,' she said after swallowing. 'This is the most amazing thing I've ever tasted. Try some.'

He smiled at her delaying tactic but took a piece and tried it anyway. It was good; light and soft and creamy with a slim layer of jam to cut through the richness.

He took another mouthful and waved his fork around in a get-on-with-it kind of way.

'OK, fine. Pops, my grandfather, is from Carwyn Bay and I'm here to find out more about my family's Welsh heritage.'

Adam tilted his head to one side and watched as Ruby shovelled more cake into her mouth.

'That's not the whole story, is it?' he said, when it became apparent she wasn't going to keep talking.

She sighed and took a swig of water. 'You're very tenacious! All right, that's not the whole story. My family is very small. There was only Mum, Dad, Grams, Pops and I until very recently. Grams and Pops have always lived with us and it was Pops who always told me a bedtime story every night as I was growing up. He had such a lovely Welsh lilt and he'd tell me these wild and wonderful legends. It's because of him that I developed a love of mythology.'

'Had?' Adam picked up on the past tense.

Ruby glanced down at her empty plate and picked up a few crumbs using her fingertip.

'Pops died in January. It was a shock to us all. He was so fit and healthy and then one day he had a heart attack. We believed he'd recover but after a few days in hospital he passed away. I know he wouldn't have wanted to linger in bad health, but we thought he had years left. I miss him so much.'

'I'm sorry,' said Adam. She nodded sadly.

'The thing was, none of us knew where he came from.'

'I thought you said he had a lovely Welsh accent,' said Adam softly.

'Oh we knew he came from Wales, we just didn't know what part of Wales. If anyone questioned him he said he didn't have any family left and that made him sad and he didn't want to

51

talk about it. In every other respect, we were all incredibly close. I was curious about his past as a child but as time went on I kind of forgot about it.'

'Why the interest now?' asked Adam.

'When Pops was dying — ' Ruby swallowed. 'He was on a lot of pain medication and he started talking to someone who wasn't there. He was very agitated. Then he mentioned Carwyn Bay and once when he was rambling he said something about Melveryn Manor. He kept saying, 'no' over and over again. One of the last things he said was, 'If you do that I'll never come back'.'

'It's all a bit tenuous,' commented Adam.

She frowned at him. 'Yes, I know. But then later, when we were sorting through his belongings, we found a letter written by someone called Charles Henry and addressed to Pops. A little bit of research showed that Charles Henry was the direct descendant of Maurice Henry and although I can't find out what happened to him, I thought here would be a great place to start my research. In the letter Charles talks about how much he's missing Pops now that Charles is at boarding school and how much he wishes he was back at Carwyn Bay with Pops. He signs off by saying he can't wait to see Pops during the Christmas break and how they must finish building the tree house in the manor gardens. It's not too much of a leap to deduce that the two of them must have been very good friends.'

Ruby sat back triumphantly.

'To summarise, then,' said Adam, ticking points off on his finger, 'your grandfather didn't want to talk about what happened when he lived here and, from the sound of things, he didn't leave here under happy circumstances. You love your grandfather but instead of respecting his wishes to leave the past alone, you've come here to dig things up.'

Ruby gasped and blinked a few times. Adam squirmed under her hurt gaze. She dropped her eyes and before he could say anything else she collected their plates and headed into the kitchen.

Adam sat still for a moment. Should he head back to his desk and the comfort of his writing? It would be easier; less confrontation than finding Ruby and apologising, and he hated confrontation. But she had looked hurt and he hadn't meant to be as cutting as he'd sounded.

He stood. He couldn't hear any sounds from the kitchen. She may have disappeared deeper into the house and looking for her would waste more precious time away from his manuscript.

He walked to the kitchen door. She was standing motionless with her hands gripping the edge of the sink.

'I'm sorry,' he said quietly. 'That was insensitive of me. I didn't mean what I said to come out as harshly as it did. It was intended as a joke but as I've often been told, I'm better at horror stories than comedy.'

'It's OK,' she said softly. 'I guess I

didn't think about it before but we are going against his wishes by trying to find out more. It's just that, for us as a family, he's died and his story has ended. By finding out about his past, a little bit of that story can continue for a while longer. It's helping us heal. Does that make sense?'

'Of course,' Adam said, relieved she was still talking to him, even though he planned to go back to his writing and not return. He wasn't good at interacting with others, as he'd just spectacularly proven. 'And I really am sorry if I upset you. Clara always tells me I'm an insensitive bore.'

'That's a bit of a harsh assessment,' said Ruby, turning to the industrial dishwasher and loading their plates into it. 'Who's Clara?'

Adam wished he'd not come over to this part of the house. He wouldn't do so again. The last five minutes had turned into a disaster. He raked his hair and cleared his throat.

'Clara was my fiancée but she isn't

any more,' he explained.

'Did you finish with her because she kept calling you names?' Ruby smiled.

He could laugh and agree and go back to his writing with her none the wiser or he could tell her the truth. The truth didn't cast him in a good light, but then she'd been truthful with him, so . . .

'Not exactly.' He leaned against the preparation table and scraped at some solidified cake mixture with his nail. 'She left me for my best friend, Nick. I get why she did it. I'm a workaholic, who left her alone a lot, and he's a great guy but . . . well . . . Anyway, there's nothing I can do about it. They're happy and they're getting married in a few weeks so it was obviously meant to be.'

He smiled at the look on her face; she looked devastated for him.

'Don't worry about me,' he said. 'I was upset at the time and it's taken me a little while to get over it, but it is for the best.'

'I don't think I could be that generous,' she said firmly.

'I wasn't at my greatest straight after it happened but now I've had time to calm down I can see that they are very well suited. Far more than Clara and I ever were.'

Her frown told him she didn't believe him, but it was true. He wasn't quite at the stage of feeling pleased for them, but he felt that would come soon. He hoped that when it did, he would get his best friend back, because he missed Nick.

If the experience had taught him anything, though, it was that he wasn't going to fall for a woman again.

4

Ruby balanced a tray in one hand and held up her other hand to knock on Adam's door. On the tray was a cup of tea and a homemade chocolate muffin.

The muffin was her best attempt yet. She'd made it with melted milk chocolate and soured cream. She'd been a bit dubious about the soured cream ingredient. Sure, it tasted great in a fajita but what was it doing in a cake? Then she'd tasted one about half an hour after she'd pulled them from the oven. The outside of the muffin had a slight crunch to it but the inside had melted all over her tongue. It was a triumph.

Her hand hovered inches from Adam's door but she couldn't bring herself to knock. After a few moments she let it drop. She hadn't seen Adam in a few days and it was all her fault.

He'd been true to his word and come

over to her side of the building to give her some much-needed cookery lessons every day for several days in a row. She hadn't made amazing progress, but he'd been very patient and nothing had caught fire so things were definitely going in the right direction. Eventually two of her Victoria sponges had been an outright success and they'd celebrated with large slices and mugs of tea on the café's outside terrace.

With the sound of the sea roaring in the background and the feel of the late spring sun on her shoulders, it had felt idyllic to Ruby, and she'd almost forgotten her real reason for staying at Melveryn Manor. As for Adam, she'd discovered something different about him every time they'd met. He was an unusual mixture; overly confident yet quite shy. When bossing her about in the kitchen he took the lead, but if she tried to talk to him about something personal he'd change the subject and ask about her life in the States.

When he wasn't bossing her about,

Ruby liked to admire the way his lean body moved around the kitchen and the effortless way he lifted heavy sacks. He was cute and he was single. She was single. They were alone in the house for the summer. It was a no-brainer to Ruby. She'd introduced a little flirting to their last encounter. So little that she thought it might have gone unnoticed; a brief brush of her hand against his and holding his gaze for slightly longer than necessary. She'd only done it to test the water, see how he'd respond. It had been a big mistake.

Adam had shut down completely and almost immediately disappeared to his rooms. The next day he hadn't turned up to help her. In fairness, he'd never said that he would come every day but when a few days passed and he didn't show up, Ruby realised how much she missed him. She'd met lots of people in the few weeks she'd been staying in Wales but he was the first one who had been becoming a friend — and she'd blown it.

But his behaviour was odd. It wasn't as if she'd asked him to marry her and to be the father of her children! She was only after a summer interlude — because whatever happened with the investigation into Pops, she was still going home to Pennsylvania at the end of the summer. She had students to teach and a research book on mythology to write. If Adam wasn't interested, she was a big girl, she could take it. His disappearance had made the whole thing a bigger deal than it needed to be.

When she'd made her first successful chocolate muffins she'd wanted to celebrate with Adam. After she'd leapt about the kitchen in triumph she'd plated one up for him. She stepped a little closer to Adam's door and listened for the sound of any movement but all she could hear was the relentless tick of a grandfather clock on her side of the house. She stepped back; she felt a little foolish standing her with a tray in her arms. She'd leave it. She'd go back to the kitchen and make another batch of these glorious muffins to sell tomorrow. Adam knew where to find her if he wanted to speak to her.

Before she could move away from the door it swung open and Adam stood before her.

'Oh,' he said, 'I didn't expect to see you there. I was coming to see how you were getting on.'

Ruby cleared her throat.

'It's all good,' she said. 'I made these.'

She held up the tray for him to see the muffin.

'It's edible. In fact it's more than edible — it's downright delicious.'

Adam grinned.

'Is that one for me?' he asked.

'Yes.' Ruby thrust the tray in his direction.

'Thanks,' said Adam, taking the tray from her. 'Would you like to come in while I try it? You can update me on your progress.'

'Sure,' said Ruby, pleased that he seemed to be his normal self again.

Hopefully he'd been keeping away because he needed to write and not because of her clumsy attempt at flirting. Even so, she would keep any flirting out of their relationship from now on. It was good to have an ally in this country and she didn't want to lose him by making him feel uncomfortable.

Ruby followed Adam into his suite. She'd not been inside since the very first time she'd met him, and then she'd been rushed through the corridor with no time to take in details. This time she walked slowly, sneaking peeks at her surroundings. From what she could tell, Adam was very neat. The few rooms they passed had no clutter at all. Ruby thought of her own tiny room, now strewn with her limited belongings. She could use a bit of neatness, but she didn't think it was in her genetic make-up. Everyone in her family was the same. It made finding things in a hurry difficult, but she wouldn't have it any other way. Home meant messiness; anything else wasn't relaxing.

Adam took her into a small sitting room, which looked as if it was never used. There were no photographs, paintings or any of his personal mementoes. It looked as if this was Adam's first time in the room as well.

'Can I get you anything to eat or drink?' he asked as he placed the tray on a small table.

'No, it's OK, thanks. I've already had two of those muffins this morning.'

'They're that good?'

'I think so,' said Ruby, suddenly very nervous about her efforts. Yes, she thought they were good but previous attempts had been almost inedible so maybe they were only good by comparison.

Adam took his time peeling back the paper casing. By the time he took his first bite Ruby's palms were damp. She rubbed them dry on her trousers and gave herself a small shake. In the grand scheme of things, it didn't matter if the muffin wasn't fit for human consumption. She was successful at her real career and cakes were trivial really — but over the last week these muffins had become her life.

Adam swallowed. 'It's good,' he commented.

'There's no need to sound so surprised.'

'You're forgetting I saw your earlier efforts.'

Ruby laughed, 'I can now make a good Victoria sponge and these chocolate muffins. My lemon drizzle cake still sinks in the middle, though, and I've had to take Spotted Dick off the menu because mine turns into a lumpy stodgy mess.'

'What are you going to do about the rest of the menu?' asked Adam, his eyes twinkling in amusement.

'I've got the savoury sections under control — especially now I understand what a butty is — and I've found an ingenious solution to the other cakes on the menu.'

'Oh?'

'According to the notes my predecessor left, the Victoria sponge is the best seller. I'm going to do a special offer on that and the chocolate muffins in order to direct the customers to those two.'

'What happens if someone desperately wants a slice of lemon drizzle? Are you going to squish two sunken ones together to try and make a whole?' Adam's eyes sparkled with suppressed laughter over his cup of tea. Even though he was making fun of her, Ruby was glad to see his amusement. He was relaxed. She had overreacted. He obviously hadn't been keeping away from her because of her flirting. She must stop being so paranoid.

'I do have a back-up plan,' she confessed.

'You do?' said Adam, grinning. 'Am I allowed to know what it is?'

Ruby shifted in her seat, 'Do you promise not to go straight to Estelle?'

Adam's grinned widened. 'I've kept your secret so far, haven't I? And you've kept mine. I promise that anything you tell me will remain between us. Is it that bad?'

Ruby leaned forward in her seat and

whispered, '*I've bought some cakes.*'

Adam threw back his head and laughed. The sight of his enjoyment made Ruby's heart sing. He didn't seem like a man who laughed a lot. Because of that, she told him details she'd sworn to herself that she would never reveal to another soul.

'I went to the shop in disguise,' she admitted.

Adam doubled over with laughter and Ruby laughed too as she told him how she'd driven to a store over an hour away and hidden her distinctive hair under a baseball cap. She'd worn a pair of jeans and a plain top, very different from the vibrant colours she preferred to wear. She skulked about in the bakery section for twenty minutes until she was absolutely sure there was no one she knew around. Then she grabbed a selection of Welsh cakes, bara brith, scones and some millionaire's shortbread and hustled as fast as she could through the tills and back out to her car.

Adam was wheezing with laughter by

the time she'd finished.

'This must be costing you a fortune,' he said when his laughter had finally died down.

'More than I intended,' she admitted.

The cash Estelle had given her to cover the cost of the ingredients had long gone and she was supplementing the rest with her wages from her real job. Estelle had told her that the money the café took generally paid for the ingredients for the rest of the summer, as well as Ruby's salary. Ruby had to hope she sold a lot!

'Has the cost been worth it?' Adam asked.

'I haven't had much time to explore the house over the last couple of days, if that's what you mean, but there are still a few rooms to look through in detail . . . and I've found a locked door.'

Ruby was insanely curious about what lay behind the door of the only room for which she didn't have the key. Did it contain the answer to all her questions, or was it a store cupboard?

'Have you asked Estelle for a key?'

'Not yet. I've been too busy baking. But I'm planning to go and see her next week to ask her. It could be nothing.'

Adam nodded and took a sip of his tea. Ruby was about to make her excuses and leave before the silence became awkward when Adam said, 'Would you like a hand tomorrow?'

Ruby glanced at him in surprise. He was concentrating fiercely on his tea and wouldn't meet her gaze. She'd hoped the muffin would ease the awkwardness around them but she hadn't been expecting this offer.

'Are you sure you have time?' she asked.

'I've just finished a major scene. I always take a few days out to mull over what happens next, so I might as well help you while I do. The manual work will give my brain a break.'

'Then I accept your offer of help, gratefully.' Ruby stood and reached for the tray. 'The doors open at ten but feel free to come over whenever you are ready.'

'I'll be there at nine-thirty,' he said.

69

'I can't tell you how much I appreciate that. I was nervous about starting off on my own.'

She made towards the door and Adam stood to follow her.

'Oh,' she said before she made it out of the room. 'But won't someone recognise you? And then your secret will be revealed.'

'I don't think I'm that much of a celebrity.'

'Your photograph is on your books.'

'I thought you didn't read my books,' said Adam, as he followed her down the corridor.

'I picked up a copy of your new paperback, *Falling Stars*, when I bought the cakes.'

'How did you get on with it?' Adam asked.

Ruby opened her mouth to say that she'd thought the story was great but then decided Adam wouldn't want empty platitudes. She told him the truth instead.

'I made it to the end of chapter one,' she said.

'Chapter one is only two pages!'

'I was desperately scared by the end of those two pages. I had to get out of bed and check I'd locked all the doors and windows. Then I got back under the covers and pulled them up over my head. I hid for the whole night.'

Adam snorted. 'Ah yes, under the bedcovers is definitely the securest place to hide. No one would think of looking for you there.'

Ruby held up a hand. 'Please don't scare me any more. You have a seriously frightening mind.'

Adam chuckled again. They'd reached the door that separated her part of the house from his. She stepped through and turned to look at him. She was reluctant to leave, but she was conscious that appearing eager for his company could frighten him off again.

'Thanks again for offering your help tomorrow.'

'It's no big deal,' he said leaning against the door jamb. 'In fact I've had an idea of something you could do tomorrow that might further your quest, and I'm curious to see how it pans out. So I'm not being entirely altruistic.'

'What plan is that?' Ruby asked, intrigued.

'Tomorrow there'll be guests from the village. I'd be surprised if there isn't at least one of them who remembers your Pops. You could ask them what they know.'

Ruby stared at Adam for a moment. He'd just suggested such a simple idea, and one which should have occurred to her. Just because Pops had wanted to keep his Welsh life a secret, it didn't mean that Ruby had to as well.

Pops was a good guy. All she had to do was ask someone what his secret was. What was the worst thing that could have happened?

5

Ruby wiped over the already immaculate kitchen surface. Everything was ready for the day. All she had to do now was wait for the customers to arrive. It was all going to be fine. At least that's what she told herself every few minutes.

'Hello,' called a voice from the kitchen door. 'Don't worry, it's only me.'

'Estelle,' cried Ruby. 'How lovely to see you.'

Ruby was surprisingly happy to see Estelle. Not that Estelle wasn't lovely, but Ruby was keeping so many secrets from her new boss that she normally felt quite guilty in her presence. Today, she was so nervous she was pleased to see a friendly face.

'I've come to see you've got everything you need,' said Estelle. 'I must say it's looking very clean and organised in here.'

Estelle pulled open the large stainless steel fridge door and peered inside. Ruby thanked her lucky stars that she'd removed all evidence of the shop-bought cakes. The flattened boxes were currently hiding under her bed. She'd have to ask Adam's advice for getting rid of them. The murderers in his books were always getting rid of bodies in ingenious ways so a few bits of card should be a simple task for his cunning mind.

'It all looks great in here — you're very neat and organised. I like the labelled plastic boxes, that will be a great time saver,' Estelle said as she closed the door and beamed at Ruby. 'I'll be up this afternoon and I look forward to sampling that delicious-looking Victoria sponge. I love your opening weekend special offer idea. That will go down a storm with our regular customers.'

Ruby smiled. 'Let's hope so.'

'I'm sorry I've not been up to visit before today. How have you found the cleaning?'

'It was all pretty easy,' said Ruby. 'My

predecessor did a good job of cleaning up before she closed up last year. The worst I found were some giant dust bunnies. There is one door I don't have the key for, though. Do you know why that would be?'

Estelle frowned. 'Are you sure?' she asked. 'Have you tried all of the keys I gave you?'

'Yes, and I'm positive. I've double, then triple checked.'

'Will you show me?' asked Estelle, puzzled.

Ruby grabbed her bunch of house keys and the two of them made their way through the house. Ruby had pinned all her hopes on what lay behind the closed door. She was expecting a treasure trove of information. It would be a blow if she'd made a simple mistake and overlooked the key among the others. What if the door opened easily to reveal rooms like the rest of the house?

She'd been through the rest of the rooms with a fine tooth comb. The scholar in her found them fascinating in relation to the author Maurice Henry, but they had been scant on any detail about the family that had lived in the house after his death until they ran out of money to pay for the upkeep.

The trustees must have removed the belongings of the last inhabitants of the house and arranged everything as it would have been during Maurice Henry's lifetime. Obviously no one in the Henry family had done anything particularly interesting since Maurice. The trustees had done an excellent job, but it was frustrating for Ruby.

She stopped at the locked door and waited patiently while Estelle went through every key.

'You're right,' said Estelle once she'd finished. 'This door doesn't open. I can't believe I've not noticed before.'

Estelle rattled the door knob as if this would miraculously open it. Then she pushed against the door. Ruby knew that wouldn't work because she'd tried both strategies before.

'I do love a mystery,' said Estelle, after she'd tried both options and failed to open the door. 'I'll see what I can find out and I'll give you a progress report this afternoon. Imagine if we find an undiscovered manuscript by Maurice Henry!'

Estelle's eyes shone with excitement and Ruby nodded. It would be great — but not as good as finding information about Pops.

'Now I'd best let you get on,' said Estelle. 'It's only an hour until opening time and I'm sure you've got things to do.'

Ruby's tummy fluttered with nerves as they headed back towards the kitchen. She wondered whether she should mention Adam's offer of help and decided she would. She was here on enough false pretences as it was; she didn't want to find out later that having an extra person in the kitchen violated some law she didn't know about.

'Adam's helping me out today. I hope that's OK,' she said in a rush.

Estelle stopped in her tracks. 'You've managed to get the reclusive writer out of his self-imposed exile!' she exclaimed.

Ruby was wary of the speculative light that had sparked in Estelle's eyes.

'He said he was at a point in his novel where he needed a break from it,' she said.

'Yes, and I'm sure doing unpaid work in a kitchen is just the thing he needs. I'm sure the decision had nothing to do with our new and very beautiful house manager.'

Estelle grinned and clapped her hands in delight. Before Ruby could argue that Adam definitely wasn't interested in her in that way, Estelle had said her good-byes and left.

Ruby felt faintly embarrassed. She hoped Estelle would keep her observations to herself. She didn't want to scare Adam off. She needed his help too much.

Wanting something to occupy her mind, Ruby put four thick rashers of bacon in a pan. She left them sizzling while she cut into two of the crusty white mini-baguettes that had been delivered that morning from the local bakery.

'Something smells good.'

Ruby jumped. She hadn't heard Adam arrive over the noise of the spitting bacon.

'I'm making breakfast. I hope you're hungry.'

Adam sniffed the air. 'I'm always ready to eat when I smell bacon. What can I do to help?'

'For the moment I only need you to talk to me; it will help keep me calm. When the customers arrive I'd be grateful if you could help me prepare the orders. I was thinking that it's probably best for you to stay in here. Is that OK? I know it's a lovely day outside and I don't want to keep you cooped up, but someone is bound to recognise you if you come out.'

From the amused expression on Adam's face Ruby realised she was rambling again. She cleared her throat and then gave him a brief tour of the kitchen. He already knew where most things were after spending so much time helping her out, but she had changed a few things round to try and make the setting more efficient.

When he assured her for the fifth time that he understood what needed to be done, they made their way to the not yet opened café.

Ruby ate in silence, enjoying the way the warm bacon had melted the butter she'd spread over the baguettes. She licked her fingers, and had to stop herself from licking the plate. She hoped her customers enjoyed her cooking as much as she did.

Adam cleared breakfast away so Ruby flitted around the café, straightening tablecloths and tweaking the plastic flowers. The opening time came and went. Twenty minutes passed and it was still only the two of them.

'This is very anticlimactic,' announced Ruby, finally returning to the kitchen.

Adam had pulled out his phone and

was flicking through some screens while sitting on a bar stool, the kitchen's only seat.

'I guess we know why Estelle only needed one person to look after the house,' said Adam, looking up at her.

'I hope all this food doesn't go to waste,' said Ruby, fiddling with the cord on the tabard she'd put on to protect her clothes. 'If you want to head off I won't mind,' she lied.

The last thing she wanted was for Adam to leave.

'Why don't I go and have a look at this mysterious locked door of yours?' suggested Adam. 'If there's time when I get back, you could tell me everything you know about your grandfather's life in Wales and then we could come up with a plan of action.' Adam stood and then paused, 'That is if you don't mind me poking my nose in.'

'Two heads are better than one,' Ruby reassured him.

Left alone, Ruby was slightly miffed with herself that she hadn't thought to come up with an action plan. So far she was winging her investigation, and all she had to show for her efforts was a photograph in a book.

She could have ordered the book online from the States. That would have been a lot cheaper than her current expenditure, but definitely not as exciting. After all, there was no reason to go undercover shopping in her home town.

The café bell tinkled, snapping her out of her thoughts and bringing her back to the present. Finally she had customers! She made her way into the café where she found a young couple standing by the counter.

'Hello,' she called. 'How can I help you today?'

'Two admissions, please,' said the man.

Ruby took their cash and rang it into the ancient till.

'I'm so excited the house has finally opened,' said the girl. 'I'm studying Maurice Henry's work this semester and I'm thinking of writing my dissertation on him next term.'

Excited to meet an English student, Ruby got into a twenty-minute discussion on the finer points of Henry's work. The girl's boyfriend smiled indulgently but when Ruby caught him glancing surreptitiously at the clock on the café's wall she let them both go.

'When you've finished your tour, do stop back here for some Victoria sponge. It's on special offer today,' she called after them.

She returned to the kitchen to find Adam back on the kitchen stool, grinning at her.

'You really know your stuff,' he said.

'Yeah,' she agreed. 'It's how I got the job. I dazzled Estelle so much she forgot to ask about my baking skills and my total lack of waitressing experience. What's that you've got?'

Ruby gestured to a book in Adam's hands. From its cover she could tell it wasn't one of his.

'I went through the library on my

way back from the locked door and found this. It's a history of the Henry family. I've read the first few pages but it's very dry and my mind keeps wandering.'

'I looked for books on the Henry family before I came here but I couldn't find anything that dealt with the family after Maurice's death.'

Ruby gently tugged the hardback out of Adam's hands and ran her hand over the cover. Her grandfather might be mentioned in it. She flicked it open, read a few lines and pulled a face.

'I see what you mean. This is deadly.'

'It's probably why you couldn't find the book online. I bet it went out of print years ago.'

'It's a great clue, though,' said Ruby. 'Well done for finding it. I don't know how I missed it.'

'You've been searching the whole house for clues. It's a broad canvas. I was only focussing on one thing.'

'Well, I look forward to . . . Oh my, there's the bell again.'

She thrust the book back into Adam's hands and headed back to the café. A large group of ramblers had chanced across the open house and claimed to be ravenously hungry. Ruby waited until they all settled in their seats before taking their order, smiling at them all as she wrote their requests on her notepad. Her smile stayed firmly in place despite her sense of growing panic. Every customer wanted something different. In all her planning scenarios she hadn't imagined this level of difference. She didn't know where to start.

She ran through to Adam and waved the order in front of him.

'Look at this,' she hissed. 'It's going to be impossible to do all this at once!'

'OK,' said Adam, taking the list from her. 'You do the drinks while I start on the sandwiches. Then come and join me when you're finished.'

Ruby was standing frozen in front of him.

'Don't look so alarmed. It really isn't difficult.'

The next two hours were a whirlwind as far as Ruby was concerned. No sooner had one customer left then another group came in. There was no time for lunch, or even time to talk to Adam other than to discuss dishes.

By mid-afternoon there was only one table of customers left, a group of women who ordered tea and Victoria sponge all round. Ruby served them and left them to it.

'I'm starving,' she announced to Adam.

'Me too,' he agreed.

'But I'm too exhausted to make anything.'

'Shall we have some of your Victoria sponge? It seems to be going down well and we want to have some before it's all gone.'

Ruby felt a swell of pride. 'It is going down well, isn't it? So much better than the shop b — ' She glanced over her shoulder. 'I mean much better than the *other ones*,' she finished in a whisper.

'The compliments you're getting

should give you more confidence in your baking ability.'

'Yes,' agreed Ruby as she pulled two clean plates out of the dishwasher. 'I'm going to perfect my lemon drizzle over the next week and after you explained how easy bara brith is to make, I'm going to give that a try too.'

Adam accepted his slice of cake and indicated that she should take the stool.

'No, please, you have it. I'm fine.'

It wasn't entirely true. Ruby ached in places she hadn't known she had muscles, but Adam was helping her out with no reward. The least she could do was offer him the only chair.

'I insist,' said Adam. 'You're the one who's done all the walking today. Please sit down.'

She sank gratefully on to it. The stool was hard but it was better than remaining on her feet.

'Estelle rang while you were serving. She's not going to make it up today but she thought you'd want to know her progress on the missing key.'

Frustratingly Adam stopped talking and took a large bite of cake.

'Is there any?' asked Ruby impatiently, waiting impatiently while he chewed and swallowed.

'Not really,' he said finally. 'No one from the trustees knows anything about it.'

'How odd,' murmured Ruby, puzzled.

'But,' said Adam, grinning, 'I think you'll like this next bit of news. Estelle is going ask Laura Henry about it. Apparently Laura is the last living member of the Henry family.'

'There's a member of the family still alive!' gasped Ruby. 'I'd assumed they'd all passed away and that was why the house was now open to the public.'

'Even better, she's in her eighties — so she must have known your Pops.'

'This is amazing, Adam.' It was better than Ruby could have hoped for. Her heart was racing as she considered the possibilities.

'Don't get too excited. Apparently she's not well and is in a nursing home.

Estelle gave me the impression she doesn't receive guests often.'

'Oh,' said Ruby, deflated. 'It's worth following up, though. Imagine if I could speak to her.'

'It's worth asking,' Adam agreed. He forked several pieces of sponge into his mouth before asking, 'Did the ladies out there have anything to say about Charles or Pops?'

'I haven't asked yet. I'll do it when I take out the bill. Do you think they are from the village?'

'They definitely are. The one nearest the wall is Mary. She runs the Post Office.'

Ruby peered into the café.

'She could be old enough to have known Pops,' she said. 'Although it's difficult to tell.'

She turned back into the kitchen to see Adam unloading clean plates from the dishwasher. She felt a wave of gratitude towards him for giving up his time to assist her. With no previous waitressing experience, the day would have been a disaster had she been left to her own devices.

'Thanks so much for helping me. I couldn't have done it all without you,' she said.

'I'm sure you could have done,' Adam said brusquely. 'It was busy, but nothing like cafés I worked in when I was a kid. Once you've sorted out a routine you'll be fine.'

Ruby was surprised by his tone, but then maybe he'd taken her thanks as a plea to come and help her again tomorrow. She hadn't meant it like that. It had been kind of him to give up a day — but giving up another when he wasn't being paid was quite another thing.

'I'll go and give the ladies their bill,' she said, changing the subject.

Adam nodded. 'I'll wait to see what they've got to say and then I'll head off.'

Ruby headed into the café and punched some numbers into the till. It took some effort to depress some of the stiff keys.

'Hello ladies,' she said as she approached their table. 'How was everything today?'

Ruby was gratified when everyone confirmed how delicious the food was and she lapped up the praise of her Victoria sponge. Her family would be amazed by her newfound cookery skills.

'You're from the States,' stated the lady whom Adam had identified as Mary.

'That's right,' said Ruby, collecting the empty plates. 'I'm from Stanmore, Pennsylvania.'

'Estelle mentioned you were over here doing some research,' said Mary. 'I've lived here all of my life so if there is anything I can help you with do let me know.'

'Actually,' said Ruby, glad for such an easy lead-in, 'I'm interested in speaking to anyone who's heard of, or who knew, Alwyn Turner.'

It felt strange to call Pops by his given name. Everyone called him Pops at home, even people not related to him.

'I knew Alwyn,' said Mary.

'How do I know that name?' asked the lady sitting next to Mary, her forehead creased in puzzled recognition.

'He's infamous around here, that's how,' said Mary with the satisfaction of someone with a good piece of gossip.

Everything slowed apart from Ruby's heart rate which accelerated rapidly.

'What do you mean by infamous?' asked Ruby, impressed that her voice sounded calm when her knees had started to shake ferociously. Infamous was not a word she would associate with her steadfast Pops.

'Alwyn Turner,' said Mary, clearly relishing her moment in the spotlight, 'is the man who murdered Charles Henry.'

6

Adam chewed the end of his Biro as he peered at a scribbled note he'd made in the margin of his manuscript. He couldn't decipher his own writing.

He held the paper up and turned it towards the window as if the extra light would make his handwriting clearer. He put the paper back down and glanced at the clock.

In fifteen minutes Ruby would be running around filling orders all by herself.

He had no intention of helping her today. Running the café was her job and writing his next book was his, and he needed to get on with it if he was to make his deadline. His gaze flicked down to his note again. It still didn't make any sense. Perhaps it would be easier to concentrate if he could just get Ruby out of his mind for a few seconds.

His study, which had once seemed like a haven of calm, felt dull and lifeless this morning. Yesterday Ruby had been a whirlwind of activity. She'd charmed customers and fulfilled orders with ease. He didn't think she'd noticed how people lingered over their coffees so that they could get another chance to talk to the vibrant young woman. She showered each guest with individual attention, learning their names with an ease he envied and talking to them as if they were lifelong friends. She'd talked almost all the customers into eating her Victoria sponge and she'd been a roaring success — right up until the point when she'd heard the shocking news about her grandfather.

Adam had been listening to her enquiries just inside the kitchen door. He stepped into the café seconds after Mary's bombshell.

Ruby had been frozen; her arms covered in plates and stacked high with detritus from the table. The women had chattered on, discussing the old scandal without realising the impact the revelation had had on Ruby.

Adam had tugged her into the kitchen and taken the plates. He'd gently sat her down on the kitchen stool and returned to the café to deal with the ladies. He'd organised their bill and lightly shepherded them to the exit once they'd paid.

By the time he'd returned to the kitchen, twenty minutes had passed and Ruby appeared to have regained control. She'd chattered non-stop to him about the customers and all the food she needed to prepare for the next day. He hadn't been able to get a word in edgeways.

Then the café door had chimed again and she'd raced out. She'd returned with a small order and assured him she could handle everything from here on. She'd all but shoved him out of the kitchen in her haste to be rid of him.

He'd tried to talk about her grandfather but she'd dismissed him with a brief, 'I can't think about that yet,' and then she'd bustled off to make two cappuccinos.

Had he not spent the day studying her, he would have assumed that she was OK — shocked perhaps, but nothing more.

Unfortunately for him he *had* spent the day watching her, even when he told himself he wasn't. She was beautiful in motion, a whirling blur of colour and laughter. And he was an idiot for taking notice of the way her hazel eyes were bright with happiness and how that brightness had disappeared after she'd been told the news about her Pops.

He was an idiot, because she was too young for him — not only in years but in temperament. She was too vibrant. He was content to sit in his room and lock the world away while he worked. She was the exact opposite. He was an idiot, because she lived in America and he was British and that kind of distance was insurmountable. And he was an idiot because he'd seen she was attracted to him and he'd run a mile. He didn't want to start something that was doomed to end before it had even begun.

He banged his head on the table. He was mostly an idiot because no matter how many times he went over the logic that argued Ruby was bad for his hard-won equilibrium, he was still going to go and see if she was all right. He promised himself that if she brushed him off again he'd come back and immerse himself in work.

He stood up and shook his head wryly. Yes, he could tell himself that's what he would do but he knew, deep down, that if he sensed in even the tiniest way that she needed him, he would stay.

He let himself into the main body of the house again and set off down the corridor. Everything was silent apart from the relentless tick of a hidden grandfather clock.

He let himself into the café and made his way to the kitchen. He stood in the doorway and looked at Ruby. She was stood at the kitchen counter looking down at her hands. At first he thought she might be crying but her shoulders were still and her breathing was even.

So as not to startle her he tapped lightly on the kitchen door. Her head snapped up and she turned towards him.

'Oh, hi, Adam. I wasn't expecting to see you today,' she said, brightly.

'Hi. I wanted to see how you were doing.'

He took a step into the kitchen. Up close, he could see purple shadows underneath her eyes.

'I'll be fine today,' she said. 'You were right about getting a routine together. I've been up for a few hours doing more baking and rearranging things so they're easier to reach, and . . . '

'It's good that you're feeling more organised but that's not what I meant and you know it. It must have been a shock to hear what Mary had to say about your grandfather. I won't talk about it if you really don't want to, but I'm here for you, if you do.'

Ruby wrapped her arms around herself and took a shuddery breath. Adam crossed his arms to stop himself from crossing the room and wrapping her in a tight hug.

'It was a horrible shock,' she whispered. 'I don't believe it's true, but why would she say such a thing otherwise?'

Adam shrugged. From all Ruby had told him about her grandfather, he didn't seem like a man who could commit murder. But what did he know? He'd never met the man, and Ruby's account of him would be hugely biased by the unconditional love she had for him.

'Have you spoken to your family about Mary's assertion?' he asked.

'No,' she said. 'They'd be devastated that such a rumour exists. Especially Grams. I texted Mom last night to tell then I was too tired to Skype them all but I won't get away with that excuse for more than a couple of days — I

don't have a reputation as a non-talker.'
Ruby managed a weak smile. 'The minute
they see me they'll know something's
up and I can't lie for toffee.

'We'll need to have something else to
tell them, then,' said Adam, roping
himself into helping her without giving
too much thought to his motivation.

Ruby glanced at him in surprise.

'What can I tell them? I'm going to
spend another day here rushed off my
feet. There's no sign of this mystery key
and I can't find any other information
in any of the rooms I can open.'

'Don't be so defeatist. It's not like
you.'

'You've not known me long,' said
Ruby, her arms tightening. 'Maybe I'm
always like this.'

Adam snorted. 'You're a whirlwind,
Ruby Turner. You've had a shock and
that's knocked your confidence, but
there's no time for wallowing if you
want to get this solved before you go
back to the States. Now, pull yourself
together and make us some breakfast

while we brainstorm ideas.'

Ruby gaped at him in surprise. Adam pulled out a crumpled notebook from his back pocket and set it down on the table. He smoothed down the paper and scribbled *Alwyn Turner* at the top. He deliberately didn't look at Ruby.

It wasn't in his nature to bark out orders like a sergeant major and he'd been raised to treat women with respect. He was pretty sure demanding breakfast went against the ethics his mother had gone to great pains to instil in him. But Ruby needed a boost to spur her back into action. He scribbled a random note underneath his heading and listened as Ruby started to move around the kitchen.

He glanced up to see her put thick cut sausages in the frying pan and his stomach rumbled.

'Was there anything in that book you found?' asked Ruby as the sausages began to sizzle.

Adam smiled at her back. She may not be back to full fighting spirit but at least she was moving forward with her investigation.

'I managed to find the section that dealt with Charles Henry's death but the author only referred to it as an 'unfortunate incident'.'

Adam straightened as Ruby flipped the sausages onto a chopping and began slicing them. He flicked on a kettle and pulled two mugs out of the cupboard.

'He was an exceptionally dull writer,' said Adam as he dumped two teabags into the mugs, 'but I find it unusual that he didn't talk about the death. If he had been murdered I'm sure even the author would have been able to sensationalise that a little. Perhaps all we're looking at here is a bit of overblown local gossip that's become twisted over time.'

'It's extreme gossip, if that's all it is,' said Ruby, picking up two plates and nodding Adam through to the café. 'Neither Alwyn or Charles are around to dispute what she said. As far as Mary was concerned, Charles' death was juicy gossip to discuss with her friends.'

They sat near the window.

'This is very good,' said Adam, holding up his sausage baguette. 'I'd never have known that two weeks ago you couldn't cook at all.'

Ruby grinned. 'Thanks. I think it's good, too. I've even developed a liking for the imaginatively named 'brown sauce'.'

Adam laughed and took a swig of tea.

'Right then,' said Ruby. 'What's your suggestion for my next move?'

Adam picked up his pen again.

'Tomorrow is Monday — the house is closed during the week. We could visit Mary when the Post Office opens and ask her for more details.'

Ruby swallowed a mouthful of her sandwich and shook her head.

'I don't want to ask her any more questions.'

Adam nodded. 'OK, we won't do anything you don't want to do — but why is it that you don't want to speak to her again?'

'I don't want to turn Pops into local gossip. It feels disrespectful — especially as he moved countries possibly to avoid this happening.'

'OK, fair enough. My suggestion then is that we call on Laura Henry,' said Adam, after swallowing another mouthful of baguette.

'I thought Estelle told you that Laura Henry isn't well and doesn't welcome guests. How will we get to see her? Especially if she gets wind that I'm the granddaughter of . . . ' Ruby's eyes turned bleak and she turned to look out of the café's windows. 'Well, you get the picture.'

'We'll just turn up and ask,' Adam stated.

'We can't do that!' exclaimed Ruby, turning back to look at him. 'Can we?'

'I've found that ringing asking permission often results in a 'no'. It's much harder to refuse a person standing in front of you.'

Ruby cupped her mug of tea in her hands.

'OK, it's worth a try. When shall we go?'

'Tomorrow.'

Ruby spluttered on a sip of tea.

'Don't we need more time to think about it?'

'What's there to think about?'

Ruby looked around wildly as if trying to find inspiration to delay their trip.

'What reason are we going to give for going to visit her? I can't very well say who I am and why I'm there. I mean, I don't believe Pops killed anyone but I don't think upsetting an elderly lady is a good thing to do.'

'I agree, so let's not upset her. In fact, I have a hard time picturing you upsetting anyone. Don't worry about what we'll say to her. I'll think of something. Making up stories is what I do, after all. If you're serious about what finding out what happened all those years ago, then tomorrow is as good as day as any. You're not going to find any answers at the bottom of a mixing bowl.'

7

Ruby flicked through her wardrobe. What did you wear on a warm summer's day when you were trying to enter a nursing home under false pretences?

She pulled out a floral print dress and held it up to the light. Perfect. Rummaging in an overstuffed drawer, she found a fuchsia scarf which picked out the pink roses on her dress and made the outfit smarter. She tied her hair back in a loose plait and lightly brushed her cheeks with blusher.

A small mirror, bolted to the wall above a rickety desk, was the only reflective surface she had in the room. She gave a little twirl and although she couldn't see her face in the reflection, she was pleased with the way her outfit had turned out. She looked smart and respectable.

She triple-checked the side door as

she locked up. Its temperamental locking system gave her the heebie-jeebies whenever she left. There was so much worth stealing from the manor, and only this flimsy door stood between its riches and the whole world. When she was as sure as she could be that the door was secure, she slid the key into her handbag and followed the cobbled path round to the front of the manor.

The driveway was long and swept up from the wide valley below before finishing in a broad circle. The circle was used as parking for guests at the weekend, but was now empty apart from a sleek, dark grey sports car. Adam was leaning against it looking towards the ocean, arms folded and expression contemplative. She wanted to trace her fingers along his broad shoulders and his jaw line. She settled on a jaunty 'hello' instead.

She was close enough to see his pupils dilate as he watched her approach. Hadn't she read somewhere that this was a sign of attraction? Or was it just down to the change in light?

'Hey,' he said softly.

She stopped in front of him and they gazed at each other for a moment. A breeze ruffled Adam's hair and she resisted an urge to smooth it flat.

'Shall we go?' asked Adam eventually.

'Yep,' said Ruby.

She cringed as she climbed into the passenger seat. Couldn't she have done better than 'yep'?

She sank into the soft leather seat. 'Oh, this is lovely,' she said as the car purred to life.

Adam smiled across at her.

'This car was my one big indulgence when my books started to sell well,' he explained.

'She's beautiful,' said Ruby appreciatively, running her hands over the soft material of the seats. 'How fast does she go?'

Adam smiled, fleetingly. 'Pretty fast. I keep meaning to take her to a race track to try her out properly but I've been so busy.' He shrugged.

Ruby relaxed as Adam pulled out of the driveway. Wales was stunning in the summer, with dramatic hillsides sweeping upwards and deep valleys spotted with opal lakes. Ruby was content to let the scenery zip past as she imagined the heroes of her favourite Celtic legends striding across the dramatic landscape.

She was so deep in her imaginary world that it was a while before she realised Adam's mood didn't reflect her own. A small frown creased his forehead and she could see that the skin around his knuckles was stretched white on the wheel.

She watched him for a few moments, hoping the mood was down to concentrating on the winding roads ahead, but he didn't relax his hold on the wheel as the road straightened out.

'Is everything all right?' she asked tentatively.

'Yes, of course,' he said, not glancing at her.

Another mile passed in silence.

'Are you sure?' she asked. 'Because if

today is taking up too much of your time, I can go on my own. Please don't feel you have to help me.'

This time Adam did glance across to her.

'Honestly, Ruby, I'm fine and taking a day off writing won't do me any harm. I could do with stopping for some coffee if you don't mind a break before we get there. I don't feel I've had enough caffeine today.'

'Of course I don't mind. I could do with a drink myself, I . . . ' She stopped before her tongue ran away with itself again. If he said everything was all right, she would have to believe him and not get nervous and start jabbering to fill the silence.

They drove through a small village and Ruby spotted a coffee shop.

'If you stop here,' said Ruby, indicating a nearby space, 'I'll jump out and get these. Do you want your usual?'

'Yes, please,' he said, as he slowed the car to a stop outside the café.

She glanced back at him just before

she pulled open the glass door of the coffee shop. The small frown was back and he was staring intently into the distance. She looked in the direction of his gaze but she couldn't spot anything that could hold his attention. Something was definitely bothering him, but it couldn't be anything she'd said or done. The question was, should she push him to reveal what was wrong or leave him be?

Back in the car, she handed him his double strength cappuccino and lifted the lid on her latte to give it a stir. She still hadn't decided on the way forward and sipped her latte in silence.

'There is something,' he said eventually.

Ruby said nothing, realising that with Adam, pushing would only make him clam up.

'This came this morning,' he said, reaching in front of her and unclipping the glove box. He pulled out a square, white envelope and handed it to Ruby. She put her coffee carton down and

111

held the stiff card with both hands. She guessed what it was before she opened it but she pulled the card out and read it anyway.

'Are you going to go?' she asked when she'd finished reading.

'I'm not sure,' he said, continuing his intense inspection of a distant object.

Ruby slid the wedding invitation back into its envelope. She looked across at him, trying to guess how he was feeling. He didn't seem upset to have received a wedding invitation to his best friend and ex-fiancée's wedding, but he wasn't himself. For once Ruby was lost for words but again her silence seemed to encourage Adam.

'I keep going round in circles,' he said. 'Nick's been my friend for so long I almost can't imagine not being at his wedding. I once thought that I'd be his best man; he was going to be mine. But now I'm not sure that I can cope with a whole day of pitying looks and comments.' Adam sighed and took a sip of his coffee. 'Then I think that worrying about that makes me selfish. Surely I can stand a day of scrutiny for him.'

'The invitation is for a plus one. Maybe you could take a hot date and then no one would think of pitying you,' said Ruby.

Adam laughed and Ruby entertained the wild hope that he'd ask her to go with him. Adam took a long swig of coffee and nodded slowly.

'I'll think about how I reply later,' he said eventually, 'but thanks for talking it through with me. It doesn't seem like such a huge deal now.'

Adam turned the key in the ignition again and pulled away from the kerb. Ruby swallowed her disappointment that he'd not suggested he take her as his plus one. But then, why would he? They hadn't known each other long. He probably had plenty of lovely female friends he could ask.

As the car purred along winding rounds lined with dry stone walls Ruby tried to get back to imagining the legends in the landscape but the images kept slipping away from her. She didn't want to admit it, but her heart felt a little bruised.

'I've come up with a cover story,' said Adam.

Ruby frowned. What was he talking about?

'For visiting Laura Henry,' Adam clarified when Ruby didn't respond.

'Oh!' she said. 'Of course. I meant to think about that yesterday but I was run off my feet all day and then when everyone was gone you should have seen the state of the kitchen. I couldn't see the surfaces for stacked plates. By the time I'd finished tidying it all away I collapsed into bed. It's exhausting being on your feet all day. If I get nothing else out of this trip to Wales, then at least I'll return home fit.'

Adam rubbed his nose. 'I'm sorry I didn't stay to help you.'

'Don't be crazy,' said Ruby. 'It's not even remotely your job to help me.' Adam looked ready to argue so she said, 'What's this cover story you've concocted for us today?'

'Have you heard of the phrase *Keep it Simple, Stupid*?' Adam asked.

'Of course I've heard of KISS. Don't try and claim that as British. It's an American acronym.'

Adam grinned. 'I wouldn't dream of it. Anyway I try and live by the KISS maxim whenever I can. In this case I think we should tell the truth.'

'Are you insane?' Ruby gasped.

Adam laughed. 'I don't mean all of it, but we're staying at the manor for the summer and want to find out more about the house's history. None of that's a lie.'

'And if she refuses to see us?' said Ruby, playing devil's advocate.

'There's a fascinating crime museum near the nursing home. It's tiny but it's a crime writer's dream. I visited it when I first moved into the manor, but I'd love to pop back there and have another look through the exhibits.'

'Hmm, is it gruesome?' asked Ruby dubiously.

'It's mostly about unsolved crimes but I suppose there are some gruesome bits.'

'Then I really hope Laura Henry agrees to see us,' said Ruby firmly.

Adam laughed. 'I forgot you were a complete wimp. I could drop you at some local standing stones. They're said to have a link to King Arthur.'

'That's much more up my street,' Ruby agreed. She leaned forward in her seat. 'Hey, is this it?'

Ruby pointed to a discreet sign tucked away in a towering Leylandii.

'Yep.' Adam turned quickly onto a neatly maintained driveway lined with tightly clipped box hedges.

A smart, Victorian-style house stood at the end of the driveway.

'Gee, even your nursing homes look like stately homes,' commented Ruby as Adam pulled into a visitor's space.

'I think this is a well-done replica,' said Adam, peering up at the building.

'Whatever it is, it's not a bad place to stay. When Estelle mentioned a nursing

home I was expecting something dreary
— but this building looks like a five-star
hotel.'

'Let's see if the inside matches the
exterior,' said Adam, unclipping his
seatbelt.

The inside hallway was wide and long
with thick, red carpet lining the floor.

'How do we get someone's attention?' asked Ruby, glancing around at
the empty space.

'I'd be surprised if . . . '

A door to their left opened suddenly
and a young woman dressed in a crisp,
red uniform stepped through.

'Hello,' she called cheerfully. 'I'm
Sian, one of the carers here. How can I
help you?'

'Hi,' said Adam, reaching out and
shaking Sian's outstretched hand. 'We've
called in to see if we can visit one of
your residents, a Laura Henry.'

Sian's eyes widened slightly. 'That
would be lovely if you did,' she said.
'She doesn't get many visitors and I do
worry that she's lonely.'

Ruby's heart tightened with guilt. She didn't want to take advantage of a woman's loneliness to get what she wanted.

'I'll go and check if she's available,' said Sian. 'Take a seat in our waiting room and I'll be right back.'

She held open the door behind her and Ruby and Adam stepped through into a spacious seating area.

'What did you say your names were?' Sian asked.

Adam gave both their names and explained that Laura Henry wouldn't know them. 'We're connected with her family home,' he expanded.

Ruby sank into a leather sofa and groaned softly. 'I feel awful,' she said when she was sure Sian wouldn't be able to hear her.

'Why?' said Adam.

'It's so sad that Laura Henry's alone and has no visitors. What if our visit makes her feel worse by raking up the past? Perhaps we should go?'

She made to push herself out of the seat, which was difficult because she'd sunk into the depths of it.

'Let's see what she has to say first. She may refuse to see us and then the decision is taken out of our hands.'

Adam came to join her on the settee and her cushion sank further, tipping her towards his thigh. She scrambled to stay upright and Adam shot her an amused glance. Ruby rubbed her hands and clamped her mouth shut; the urge to start talking about nothing was overwhelming.

Surprisingly Laura Henry was keen to meet her unexpected guests. Sian led them through a series of long, airy corridors to her room, stopping before entering.

She said in a low voice, 'Laura really is very unwell. She can probably only manage a short visit. I'll be back soon to see how you are getting on with her.'

'Thank you,' said Ruby, who was seriously regretting having come. It was too late; to back out now would make the situation worse, so she stepped into the room.

Laura Henry lay, propped up on

some pillows, in a large bed facing the gardens.

'Hello,' said Ruby tentatively.

'Hello, my dears,' said a soft voice. 'Do come in and take a seat.' Long fingers gestured to a small double seat to the right of the bed.

Ruby and Adam walked quietly to the seat, Ruby's guilt intensifying with every step. She perched on the edge of the hard chair and took a long look at Laura Henry.

She was very thin with a shock of short, white hair. Her owl-like eyes were a deep, chocolate brown against her creamy skin.

Adam sat next to her, his thigh touching hers in the confined space.

'Tell me,' said Laura. 'How are my beloved gardens at Melveryn? I do miss them, especially at this time of year.'

Ruby sagged slightly in relief. This was something she could talk about without fear of upsetting anyone. She loved the gardens at the manor. They were apparently small for a manor house but they were perfectly formed. Ruby described how the rose garden was slowly unfurling in the summer sun.

She only realised she had been going on for some time when she felt Adam's leg tensing.

Sian was standing in the doorway; surely their time wasn't up already. Ruby hadn't asked any questions of her own yet.

'Is everything all right, Miss Henry?' asked Sian.

'Yes, thank you.' Laura turned slightly to face Sian. 'Ruby here has been telling me all about my lovely garden. She's really brought it to life for me. I could almost smell my favourite Sunsprite rose and feel the sea air in my hair again.'

Sian smiled. 'OK then, I'll leave you for a bit longer but if you get tired, ring the buzzer.'

'I haven't felt this awake in a while,' said Laura, smiling at Ruby.

Ruby twisted her fingers on her lap. She couldn't possibly ask Laura about her brother's death. It would spoil this lonely lady's lovely mood.

Sian left and Laura turned back towards them. 'Now then,' she said. 'You haven't come here to talk to me about a garden, have you? What is it that I can help you with?'

Ruby was all for saying that they were just curious about the house and then leaving, but Adam was having none of it.

He leaned forward and said, 'We're staying at the manor, Miss Henry, and there's very little about its occupants' more recent history. We were hoping you could help us out and supply us with some background information.'

Laura nodded slowly and slid her gaze to the view of the nursing home's garden.

'Hardly anyone wants to know about that,' she said quietly. 'None of us are as interesting as the great Maurice.'

'Everybody's interesting,' said Adam sincerely.

Laura smiled sadly. 'That is true,

young man,' she said. 'But no one's interested in a group of people who did nothing with their lives apart from live well and prosper. My brother, now he was someone destined for greatness. Maybe he would have given the Henry name a boost, but we'll never know. His life was brutally cut short when he was murdered before he was twenty.'

8

The room spun slightly. Ruby gripped the edge of the couch. Adam's fingers brushed the back of her hand, reminding her that she wasn't alone. He was here with her and he would lend her the support she needed to get through this.

'I'm very sorry to hear about your brother,' he said gravely. 'Were you close?'

Laura nodded. 'We were, even though I was almost ten years older than him. We were cut off from the rest of the town living that far away from everyone, so we turned to each other for company. When he was born I used to dress him up as if he was one of my dolls.' Laura chuckled quietly. 'Poor Charles.'

Ruby was all for leaving it there. When she'd heard about Charles' death, all she could think about was how her grandfather must be innocent of the crime and how the charges against him were a complete fabrication, but now there was a victim. And not just any victim, but a young man who was loved by his sister and who'd been a cute baby. She didn't think her heart could take it. She sucked in a breath to announce that it was time for Adam and her to go but stopped when Adam gripped her hand.

'Would you like to tell us about your brother?' asked Adam gently.

'If you've time to hear the story,' said Laura, obviously sensing Ruby's desire to leave.

'Yes,' Ruby squeaked, 'we have time.'

'It's been a long time since I've spoken about Charles,' said Laura. 'I miss him so much, yet sometimes I can't remember his voice. I wish we'd been born in the time of mobile phones so that I could have taken some videos of him, but all I've got is a handful of photographs.' She tugged feebly at a drawer beside her bed. 'Perhaps you'd

be so good as to open this for me, dear,'
she said to Ruby.

Ruby felt as if she was wading
through mud as she stood to pull open
the drawer. Now she was going to have
to see photographs of this young man.
Today couldn't get any worse.

The photographs were at the top of
the drawer, suggesting they were looked
at frequently. She pulled the bundle out
and handed them to Laura.

'Thank you, dear,' said Laura, lightly
stroking the bundle. 'This is all I've got
left of him.'

Ruby was close to tears. In a minute
she would have to leave before she
started sobbing. Laura pulled the top
photograph out of the elastic band
holding them together and handed it to
Adam.

'This is Charles, on the cliff top
outside Melveryn. It was taken a year
before he died.'

Adam studied the photograph and
then handed it to Ruby. She looked
down at a black and white picture of a

thin man with a wide smile. His hair was standing up on end, caught in a brisk breeze.

'Charles had a poetic soul. He was always scribbling verses. My father had great hopes for him becoming a poet of renown, but after his death we couldn't find a shred of evidence that he'd ever written anything at all. I searched for years but I stopped in the end because I could see my behaviour was hurting Father.'

Laura pulled out another photograph. 'This one is of him with his childhood sweetheart, Jeanne.'

Charles had his arm around Jeanne, who was nearly the same height as him with short dark hair and a smile that lit up her entire face.

'I've no doubt they would have married,' said Laura. 'They'd already been together three years when this was taken. I think he was waiting until Jeanne turned nineteen before he asked her. Jeanne and I were with him on the day he died.'

Laura flicked towards the bottom of the pile.

'This one was taken an hour before we headed out on the dreadful trip,' she said. 'I'm the scrawny one at the front. The couple are obviously Charles and Jeanne.'

She handed over the photograph to Ruby, who gripped the edges and tried to steady her breathing as she heard Laura say, 'The man in the background is Charles' best friend, Alwyn.' Laura paused but Ruby knew what she was going to say next. 'He's also the man who killed him.'

Ruby concentrated on breathing in and out slowly. Her vision filled with tears as she looked at the group of young people smiling at the camera, completely unaware that all of their lives would be changed irreversibly by the end of the day.

'Everyone looks so happy in the picture,' said Adam gently. 'What happened?'

Ruby sucked in a breath. How could

he be so calm? She wanted to run from the room and forget that the last few days had ever happened. She should never have come to Wales. She should have left Pops' memory alone.

'It was a beautiful summer's day,' said Laura. 'The sun's warmth was tempered by the lightest of breezes. We'd all grown up around the coast and sailing was second nature to us. We decided to take a boat to a secluded beach further down the coast. None of the tourists knew about it and you couldn't get to it by land. We thought of that beach as our very own slice of Wales.

'We took a picnic with us. I can still taste the pork pie I ate on the boat. Food never tasted as good afterwards. Charles and Alwyn were in charge of the boat. It was a perfect day for sailing. The sea was nearly still and I remember lying back in the boat and gazing up at the nearly empty sky. It was almost completely blue with only the lightest wisps of couldn't against the dramatic colour. It was the most at peace I've ever felt.

'When we arrived at the cove the boys wanted to carry on sailing but Jeanne and I wanted to sunbathe. In the end they agreed to stop and let us off so that they could sail on for a bit. They promised to be back in time for lunch. That was the last time I saw Charles. We didn't see the boat for two hours and when he finally came back, Alwyn told us that Charles was dead. I knew straight away that Alwyn had killed him.'

Ruby cleared her throat.

'How did you know?' she asked softly.

'I didn't see it happening, if that's what you're asking, but I know deep down that he did it. Alywn was wildly jealous of Charles even though they were best friends.'

'Because Charles was going to inherit the manor?' asked Adam.

'I'm sure that was part of it but not all of it. There was also Charles' education. Charles was sent to an exclusive boarding school in England while Alwyn had to settle for the tiny local school, which taught most of its children in the same room despite the wide range of age differences. Apart from English, Alwyn was better at most subjects so his inferior education must have rankled. But the major problem was Jeanne.

'All the girls in town loved Alwyn. He was athletic, handsome and funny, even I had a brief passion for him myself despite the fact he was so much younger than me. The only girl not falling over him was Jeanne. She only had eyes for Charles and that drove Alwyn crazy with jealousy. That fateful summer they were arguing all the time.'

Ruby's legs were shaking. She couldn't reconcile this portrait of her grandfather with the man she had known. Pops had been laid back to the point of being almost horizontal. It was a family joke that the house could fall down around him and Pops wouldn't get upset. He also loved Grams with his whole heart. He'd always said she was the only woman for him. Could this really be the same man driven crazy with jealousy?

'Two days before that boat ride,' Laura continued, 'I overheard the end of a vicious argument. I heard Charles shout, 'If you tell Jeanne I will never forgive you.' Alwyn replied, 'If you don't tell her, I'll have to do something drastic and you won't like that.' I've never doubted that Alwyn killed my brother. Not once.'

9

The solid door was heavy and difficult to pull open. Adam wondered whether this was a sign that he should turn around and go home.

After one last tug it opened with a pop, sending him staggering backwards. Obviously a sign from the universe that Adam should go through with what could be a very awkward few hours.

He stepped into the pub and instinctively lowered his head to avoid smacking it against the wooden beams that ran across the ceiling. Perhaps Nick wouldn't turn up. Then Adam could have a pie and chips and maybe a pint, and convince himself that he'd made enough of an effort towards repairing his oldest friendship.

As his eyes adjusted to the dim light of the room he noticed there was only one other occupant in the pub: Nick.

Seated in the back corner facing the door, he was watching Adam's entrance intently. When Adam caught his eye, Nick nodded in acknowledgement. No backing out now.

Slowly Adam made his way over to his friend. Although it had only been six months since they'd last seen each other, he had been expecting Nick to look older. His short brown hair was still thick with a hint of a wave that he always tried desperately to subdue.

Nick was trying to appear relaxed. His long, thin legs were thrust out in front of him and his arm rested on the back of the nearest chair. Two things gave away the state of his mind; the tight hold he had on his pint, and the fact that he had a pint in the first place. Nick didn't drink much and never in the day.

The pint was almost gone and Adam smiled. At least he wasn't the only nervous one.

'Another?' he said, nodding towards the drink.

'Yeah — thanks.'

Adam ordered two pints of Funnel Blower and, because he was starving after having driven to Bristol on nothing but a slice of toast, a steak and ale pie with a large portion of chips.

Nick downed the remainder of his pint as Adam approached. 'Thanks,' he said, as Adam slid the new beer towards him.

'How's things?' asked Adam, reluctant to get to the heavy stuff straight away.

'Good, thanks,' said Nick.

The two men paused. Adam met Nick's eyes and suddenly the two of them were laughing.

'I don't think I've ever heard you so polite,' said Adam, when they'd calmed down.

'Yeah, sorry about that,' said Nick, taking a long sip of his pint. 'I'm not sure if you're about to punch me and I don't want to provoke you. You're bigger than I am. Plus I deserve it — so honour dictates that I don't protect myself.'

Adam smiled sadly at his friend.

'I'm not going to punch you,' he said. 'I never had any intention of doing so — not only because you're a policeman and I don't want to get arrested.'

Nick's lips twitched. 'I wouldn't blame you if you did. Actually it might make me feel less of a rubbish friend if you weren't being so reasonable.'

Adam studied his pint intently.

'You've never been a rubbish friend. You and Clara fell in love. You're better for her than I was and I'm glad you're making each other happy.'

Nick cleared his throat.

'Thanks,' he said eventually.

'Now we've got the mushy stuff out of the way, can we agree to never talk about it again?' asked Adam.

Nick coughed out a laugh. 'I'm more than happy to do that.'

The barman brought over a plate piled high with chips and a steaming pie and put it in front of Adam. Nick reached over to swipe a few chips but Adam whipped it away from him.

'Get your own,' he growled.

'I'll do that,' said Nick, heading to the bar and leaving Adam to cover his chips with salt. He prodded the top of the pie with his fork. Thick gravy oozed out; Adam's stomach rumbled.

'How's the writing going?' asked Nick as he sat back down, dropping some wrapped-up cutlery and packets of condiments on the table. He also set down another pint of beer. Adam had only planned on having the one, but now a second was in front of him he couldn't resist.

'Good,' he said, swiping a ketchup sachet.

'Has Detective Grimes solved the mystery?'

'He's about to.'

'Good old Grimes,' said Nick fondly. 'How many people have you killed off this time?'

'You'll have to read it to find out.'

'Will you send me a copy?' asked Nick.

That Nick had to ask was a sign of

how much their relationship had drifted.

'Do you think you'll have time to read it with everything else going on?' asked Adam.

He was skirting dangerously close to Nick's upcoming wedding and he wasn't ready to talk about that yet. He wanted to enjoy his meal first.

'I always have time for Grimes,' said Nick. 'I only wish I was as good at my job as he is.'

Adam smiled. Nick was good at his job, but real policing was a world away from Adam's fictional scenarios. Nick read Adam's early drafts and kept them as close to reality as possible by pointing out any glaring errors.

They'd met eighteen years ago at a crime writing convention. Adam had already tried his hand at writing a few novels but was getting nowhere. Nick was a young constable who'd come to give a talk on real-life policing methods. The two hit it off and stuck together as their careers progressed. It was only the events with Clara that had put a spanner in the works. Their friendship might never be the same, but hopefully they could move forward.

'Anything new in this one?' asked Nick, as his own plate of food arrived.

'I've given Grimes a love interest,' admitted Adam.

'Really?' said Nick, raising an eyebrow. 'I thought he was too hard-bitten for love.'

'I thought someone sparky might liven him up a bit,' said Adam.

'Sparky, huh? Based on anyone we know?' The corner of Nick's mouth rose in a half-smile.

Adam wished he'd kept his mouth shut. He scratched his neck and hoped the dim light of the pub would hide his blush.

'Nope,' he said and bit into his pie. He savoured the rich gravy as it spread over his tongue and ignored Nick's quizzical look.

'Are you blushing, mate?' asked Nick.

'Nope,' said Adam again.

He would never admit it, even on pain of death, but Grimes' new love interest did hold a startling resemblance to Ruby. Not in looks; he didn't want to get sued if she ever got beyond chapter one and discovered herself in his book. Like Ruby, though, his female protagonist was warm and vibrant; people were drawn to her. She was feisty too — she didn't give up on a problem when it started to prove too difficult.

That parts of Ruby's personality were appearing in Adam's book didn't mean anything, though. She was on his mind a lot because of the mystery he wanted to help her solve — and not because he was falling for her or anything ridiculous like that.

Nick didn't push. Adam knew this was because of their recent history, not because his friend believed him. Normally Nick would push until Adam told him whatever he wanted to know, pretty quickly because Nick was good at interrogating people. Today he seemed content to carry on eating his pie.

Adam scraped his plate, mopping up gravy with the last of his chips. Now he'd finished it was time to talk about the elephant in the room.

'So — thanks for inviting me to the wedding.'

Nick paused, fork halfway to his mouth.

'I'll be honest,' he said cautiously, 'it was Clara's idea. I thought you wouldn't want the awkwardness of deciding whether or not to come but she believed you should be given the option. I'm sorry if it was a crass thing to do.'

'You can tell Clara that it was the right thing to do,' said Adam, putting his knife and fork down on the plate and pushing it all to one side. 'You can also reassure her that I won't be coming.'

Nick put a full fork back down on his plate.

'Oh. I thought, at least I hoped, that . . . '

Adam held up his hand. 'Sorry, that

came out blunter than I intended. It's not that I don't want to be there for your big day and it's not that I'm not happy for the both of you. Believe it or not, I am. I was shocked to begin with and I'm sorry I said some things to you both that were hurtful. Now I'm calmer I can see how well-suited you are, far better than she and I ever were. I can honestly wish you a long and happy life together.'

Adam was pleased to feel that he wasn't just saying this; he was genuinely content with what had happened. If Nick hadn't fallen for Clara and swept her off her feet, then he would be married to her by now and they would probably be making each other quietly miserable.

'Then why won't you come?' asked Nick.

'It's Clara's big day,' he said simply.

'What about me?'

Adam grinned. 'We both know the wedding is not about you.'

Nick smiled reluctantly.

142

'I'm not coming because I think your other guests will focus on the fact that I'm there and that will distract from Clara's and your enjoyment. The day should be about you both, not about people watching to see whether I'll try and stop the wedding or get so drunk that I start shouting obscenities.'

Nick snorted. 'I'd like to see you do something so outrageous.'

'I can be outrageous!'

'Adam, you're one of the most focused, controlled men I've ever met. You say you said hurtful things to Clara and me at the beginning, but I don't remember that. My recollection is that you were very calm and considered. We both would have preferred it if you *had* got drunk and shouted obscenities at us.'

Adam sat back and fiddled with a packet of salt. Did Nick's description make him sound boring? Annoyingly his mind turned to Ruby again. No one could accuse her of being dull. If she thought nothing of crossing half the world to find out about her grand-father's past then she probably wouldn't have stood calmly by as her best friend went off with her fiancé.

He shook his head; why wouldn't Ruby stay out of his thoughts for more than a few minutes?

'I won't come to the wedding but I've got a gift for you in the car. You mustn't forget to take it,' he said, wrenching his mind away from Ruby.

Nick put his head in his hands and groaned.

'I wish you would stop being so *nice*.'

'If it makes you feel any better, I've got an ulterior motive for meeting up with you today.'

Nick looked at him through his fingers.

'You have?'

'Yes — two, actually.'

'Surprisingly that does make me feel better. What can I help you with?'

'I'm interested in the details of a very old murder case. I've tried the usual routes but come up with nothing.

Could you look into it for me?'

'Sure. What are the details?'

'At some point in the 1950s, or possibly even the very early 1960s, a man called Alwyn Turner allegedly murdered his best friend, Charles Henry. Those are all the details I have.'

'It's not a comprehensive list of information, is it? You say allegedly, so was Turner found guilty?' Nick pulled a small notepad out of his pocket.

'What I've told you is, unfortunately, all I know. If Turner did spend time in prison it wasn't for long. He was in America by 1964 and getting married to Dawn Clark in Stanmore, Pennsylvania.'

'OK,' said Nick, 'it's not much to go on but I'll see what I can do. What's the second thing?'

'There was a possible witness to the event and I'd like to track her down. Her name is Jeanne. She was living in Carwyn Bay in the 1950s and was probably eighteen when Charles Henry died.'

'Ah. Well, that really helps,' said Nick, looking up from his notepad and raising his eyebrows.

Adam laughed. 'If it was easy I wouldn't need to ask you.'

'Fair enough,' said Nick, closing the pad. 'I'll see what I can do but don't get your hopes up. There isn't a lot to go on.'

'Thanks. Any little thing will be better than what I've got at the moment.'

They sipped their pints. It felt to Adam that no bad words had ever been spoken between them.

'Will you go back to Wales today?' asked Nick.

Adam thought about Ruby alone in the house and then about the two pints he'd had. Even if he left for home later, he wouldn't feel comfortable knowing that he'd been drinking at lunchtime. Ruby didn't need him there; she had her own agenda so he needn't feel responsible for her.

'Probably not,' he said reluctantly.

'I've got the rest of the day off. I

know a pub not far from here where you can stay the night. It also has a beer garden where we can spend the rest of the day.'

'Sounds like a good plan,' said Adam.

'You're welcome to come and stay with Clara and me but maybe you'd prefer not to,' said Nick.

Adam imagined a breakfast scene with him, Clara and Nick in their pyjamas.

'Might be too soon, mate,' he said. 'Let's go and check out this beer garden of yours.'

* * *

Several hours, pints and a couple of games of pool later Nick and Adam lay slumped in reclining chairs basking in the fading light of the evening sun. Adam had switched to water an hour ago but he was feeling relaxed in the way only a few beers on a sunny afternoon can make you feel. He and Nick had talked about everything and nothing, as they always did. All was well with the world.

'Who's Ruby?' asked Nick, after a few moments' silence.

'Huh?' grunted Adam, surprised out of his moment of contentment.

'You've mentioned the name Ruby a lot.' Nick kept his face turned away so Adam couldn't tell if he was amused or simply curious.

'She's a friend.'

'Uh-huh,' said Nick.

They fell into silence once again.

'A good friend?' asked Nick eventually.

'I've only met her recently,' said Adam.

'I see.' This time there was no mistaking the underlying laughter in Nick's voice.

'It's not like that,' protested Adam.

'I never said it was.'

'Ruby's very young.'

'How young?'

'Thirty, I think.'

'So not that young then,' commented Nick.

'Too young for me,' said Adam stubbornly.

'So it is something you've considered?'

'I'd have to be blind not to. She's beautiful and funny and feisty.' The beers he'd had took control of Adam's voice, making him say something he'd rather have kept inside.

'I see. So you've met a beautiful young woman whom you're talking about all the time and you expect me to believe it's 'not like that.''

Adam snorted, 'She is lovely but it's not happening. She's also American.'

'You're always in America with your work. You like Americans so I still don't see what the problem is. And,' said Nick, seeing that Adam was about to protest again, 'this is the happiest I've seen you in a long time. You've laughed and smiled more this afternoon than I think you have in the last few years. Whatever is or isn't happening with Ruby is good for you.'

'She's fun to be around. That's it,' said Adam and changed the subject to Nick's younger brother and his new baby.

Nick didn't press him on Ruby, and Adam was glad. Their friendship was still healing and although today had gone well, he didn't want to tell his friend the real reason he didn't want to get involved with Ruby. If he allowed himself to fall for Ruby in the way he thought was possible, then she would have the power to hurt him far more deeply than Clara ever had. He didn't think his heart could cope with such a bruising.

10

The doorbell to the manor house's side door sounded at the same time as the timer pinged on the oven. Ruby was torn, but settled for pulling the oven door open. It was more important to get the cake out at the right time than to find out who had come to see her.

It wouldn't be the delivery people, as they'd already been this morning. The two most likely candidates were Adam and Estelle. Perhaps Estelle had come about the missing key; she'd not heard anything about that yet. Surely it couldn't take too long to find out what was in that mysterious room. Someone must know.

'Come in,' she yelled, as she set the cake on a wire rack.

She heard the door open but she still couldn't make out who it was. She expected Estelle but hoped for Adam.

She hadn't seen his car the day before and it hadn't been parked on the driveway this morning so he must have spent the night somewhere. Ruby had spent far too long agonising on where he might have gone. Tossing and turning last night, the image of him spending the night with a woman had haunted her.

'Something smells amazing,' said a welcome voice from the doorway.

He was carrying a rucksack over one shoulder and a parcel in one hand. He'd obviously come to see her as soon as he'd returned from wherever he'd been, instead of going over to his side of the house first. Surely that was a good sign.

'It's a disaster,' said Ruby, smiling as she pulled off her oven gloves.

'Oh. Is it meant to look like that?'

Ruby snorted. 'How many cakes have you seen in the shop with a sunken middle?'

The corners of Adam's lips twitched as they did whenever he was trying to suppress a smile. Ruby loved provoking that reaction.

'What's it meant to be?' he asked.

'Lemon drizzle cake. I can guarantee it will taste amazing but no one's going to buy something that has, essentially, imploded,' she said.

'How many have you made?'

'Five this week but four the week before, so that makes nine in total.'

'Are they all like this?'

'Yep.'

Adam still didn't laugh but Ruby could tell it was a struggle. She felt laughter bubbling up inside her too along with the desire to brush her fingertips over his lips. She pulled a cake tin towards her, keeping her hands occupied and away from any inappropriate touching.

'Here,' she said, pulling the lid off the tin, 'try a little piece of one I made earlier.'

'Honestly,' she said, when he hesitated, 'it tastes much better than it looks.'

Tentatively Adam took a small piece.

'Are you sure about this?' he asked.

'I'm not going to poison the only friend I've got in Britain,' she said. 'Try it. Go on, I dare you.'

He grinned and popped the piece in his mouth.

'Mmm,' he murmured, 'that does taste a lot better than it looks.' He reached into the tin and took out a larger chunk. 'It's lovely. It's very lemony and incredibly moist.'

'I know!' cried Ruby. 'I've followed the recipe to the letter and I can't understand why it keeps sinking in the middle.'

'Maybe it's too moist. You could try putting slightly less lemon in it next time.'

Ruby tilted her head and looked at her sunken cake. 'OK, I'll give it a go. Would you like to stay for some bara brith? I made that this morning and unlike my lemon cake, it was a total success. We could take a couple of slices out to the veranda, if you've time to stay.'

'I'd love some bara brith and I've plenty of time. There are a couple of things I wanted to talk to you about.' Adam dropped his rucksack to the floor, placing his parcel on top.

Ruby's heart started to race. What could he possibly want to discuss? Then she scolded herself. He probably wanted to chat about Pops, nothing more. Adam seemed to have developed an interest in Pops' life almost as keen as her own. She mustn't think it was anything more than that. To do so would bring unnecessary heartbreak into her life.

Outside, the sun was drying out an early morning shower. The smell of roses hung heavy in the air and the ever-present rumble of the sea sounded in the background. They chose seats which faced the coastline and Adam placed the tray on the table. Ruby sat down and began to unload the plates and teapots from the tray.

She glanced at Adam. His face was turned towards the sun and the light picked out tiny ginger spikes amongst the dark of his stubble. They glinted as he reached for the teapot and began to pour them both a cup. Ruby tore her gaze away and concentrated on her spreading butter across her fruit cake.

'How are you feeling after Monday's revelations?' asked Adam, referring to their trip to see Laura Henry.

'I spent Tuesday feeling a bit numb,' Ruby confessed. 'I couldn't help but feel immensely sorry for Laura and her loss and I almost got to the point where I thought about not going any further with my investigation. After a night of tossing and turning I began to see things in a new light. Laura obviously adored her brother and she honestly believes that Pops killed him. But I know Pops better than she did and I know, without a shadow of a doubt, that he would never have killed someone, not for any reason in the world. When I thought about this in more detail, I decided I needed to hear what other people have to say about the whole thing. The next step, I think, is to find other witnesses. If I can piece together different points of view, I might be able to get a bigger picture as to what happened. One that isn't so one-sided on either side. It would be great if I could get hold of the girlfriend — Jeanne.'

'I'm glad you said that, because I think I've found her,' said Adam.

Ruby dropped her cake in surprise.

'You have?'

'On my way back from Bristol today I stopped at the Post Office to pick up a parcel. I spoke to Mary — or rather, I should say Mary spoke to me.'

'What do you mean?' asked Ruby, thinking of the lady who'd taken so much pleasure in gossiping about Pops when she had first asked about his past.

'I promised you I wouldn't talk about Pops to anyone in the village and I had no intention of doing so but when I picked up the package that was waiting for me, she brought up the subject.'

'I see,' said Ruby.

'She asked if you were still interested in the events surrounding Charles' death. I said you were more interested in any information about Alwyn Turner, but she didn't know anything about him other than . . . well, you know. She does, however, know what happened to Jeanne.'

Ruby leaned forward.

'She married and is now Jeanne Willson. She lives on the outskirts of Carwyn Bay in a tiny village. Mary gave me very detailed instructions on how to find her house. I drove past it on my way back here, and it's not far away. I can take you, if you like.'

Ruby's heart began to pound.

'When?' she asked.

'This afternoon, if you like,' said Adam. 'I'd need to shower and change my clothes. I hadn't intended to stay in Bristol yesterday.'

Ruby's heart sank. It sounded as if he had spent an impromptu night with a woman. What other reason could he have for not coming home?

'Is everything all right?' asked Adam when she didn't respond about this afternoon.

'Yes, of course.' Ruby attempted a

smile. 'This afternoon would be great. Thank you so much.'

He frowned at her. She obviously wasn't giving off the right signal. She attempted another smile but it obviously didn't work because his frown deepened. He popped the last of his bara brith into his mouth and chewed thoughtfully.

'You said there were two things you wanted to talk about. What was the other?' she asked.

She had no right to feel this awful about Adam spending the night with a woman. He was being a great friend towards her, and it wasn't his fault if he didn't find her as attractive as she found him. Yet the thought still made her feel sick, whether she had a right to or not.

'Oh yes — that,' said Adam, suddenly becoming very interested in the teapot in front of him. 'Well, you see . . . I saw Nick yesterday.'

'Nick!' gasped Ruby, the sudden relief causing her to flop back in her chair.

'Er, yes, Nick,' said Adam, obviously a bit confused by her behaviour of the last few minutes. 'Anyway, I told him I wasn't going to go to his wedding. I thought I would be an object of too much curiosity. It might detract from them.'

'That's generous of you,' said Ruby, resisting the urge to dance for joy around the garden.

'It's a week on Friday,' he said, his gaze fixed resolutely on the same teapot. 'So . . . I was wondering if, that is if you're not too busy, whether you would like to spend the day with me.'

Ruby stilled. She hadn't expected this. It appeared Adam was holding his breath. She could hear the buzzing of bees among the roses.

'Of course, I'd love to,' she said.

'Great,' said Adam, taking his attention off the teapot and focusing instead on a napkin.

'Even to the crime museum,' said Ruby bravely.

Adam grinned and finally looked up at her. The faint blush covering his cheeks gave her hope. It might mean that he wanted to spend the day as something more than just friends.

'I'm sure we can come up with something better than that,' he said. 'I was thinking — ' He stopped as his phone rang. 'Can you hold on a moment? I'd better take this.'

With a light heart, Ruby took the dirty cups and plates back to the kitchen leaving Adam to conduct his conversation in privacy. She all but skipped to the dishwasher. Adam wanted to spend the day with her; she felt she'd won the lottery. No matter how strongly she told herself not to read too much into it, she couldn't help the joy bubbling up inside her.

'Hey.' Adam came into the kitchen. 'That was Nick. I hope you don't mind, but I asked him to do some digging on your grandfather.'

'Did he find anything?' Ruby was in such a good mood she wouldn't have minded if Adam had asked the whole of Britain to help.

'There's no record of an Alwyn Turner serving time in prison for murder,' said Adam.

'That's great news, isn't it?' asked Ruby. 'Why are you looking so serious?'

'Well,' said Adam, scratching the side of his head, 'there is a record of someone by that name serving time in prison around the dates we're looking at.'

'Oh.' Ruby leaned on the stool. 'What for?'

'Manslaughter,' Adam told her.

11

Jeanne Willson's bungalow stood in the corner of a small cul-de-sac. From her vantage point in Adam's car Ruby tried to peer through the front windows. A huge ornamental pear tree got in the way of her view but a grey car was parked on the gravel driveway, so somebody was probably in.

'Do you want to knock on the door or do you want to stare at it for a bit longer?' asked Adam.

'Ha ha,' said Ruby, poking her tongue out. 'It feels weird knowing that maybe someone inside that small house knew Pops when he was a young man. I'm trying to get my head around it.'

Thinking about it wouldn't get the problem answered. She unclipped her seatbelt. 'Let's go,' she said decisively.

She was out of the car and striding up the driveway before Adam had even opened his door. Now that she'd made the decision to get going, she wanted the initial meeting over with. Adam caught up with her as she pressed the doorbell.

'You're not slow when you put your mind to something, are you?' asked Adam, his eyes glinting with laughter.

Ruby grinned. She was glad he was with her. It seemed less serious when they were together. When she was left alone, she started to worry about how Grams and her parents would take the news that Pops had somehow been involved in a death. It would hit Grams hard, but it would probably be worse for Mom who'd idolised her father. In the few days since she'd learned about Pops, she'd managed to avoid telling her family anything. She wouldn't get away with it much longer. The more she dodged questions, the more suspicious they would become.

At least manslaughter didn't sound quite as bad as murder, but it still wasn't news they would enjoy hearing

— and she would hate hurting them, especially as they were already mourning Pops.

The door opened and a tall woman with short, grey hair worn in a bob stood before them.

'Well now,' she said, looking Ruby up and down, 'there is not a shadow of a doubt in my mind that you are a Turner. You're the absolute spit of Ann Turner. Tell me I'm not wrong.'

'My name's Ruby Turner,' said Ruby, never having heard of being related to anyone called Ann.

'Of course it is,' said the woman, nodding briskly. 'I'm Jeanne Willson. I knew the Turners very well, back in the day. But it's been a long time.'

Jeanne thrust out a hand for Ruby to shake. It was warm and dry and Ruby felt her own hand gripped tightly in a firm shake.

'And you are?' Jeanne asked, as she dropped Ruby's hand and turned to Adam.

'I'm Adam Jacobs,' said Adam,

proffering his own hand.

'Like the author. I love his stuff.'

Adam caught Ruby's eyes and winked.

'Now what can I do for you both?' enquired Jeanne.

'I'm Alwyn Turner's granddaughter,' said Ruby, deciding the direct approach was best for this woman.

'Are you now? No wonder you look so much like his mother, then,' said Jeanne, gazing down at Ruby from her advantage of the doorstep. After a long moment she held the door open wider. 'You'd best come in, then, and tell me the reason why you're here.'

★ ★ ★

Adam and Ruby stepped into the corridor and onto a tightly patterned 1970s carpet. Ruby tugged off her shoes and abandoned them by the front door. If this carpet had survived in such good condition for so long, then it deserved some respect. Adam toed his shoes off too and they followed Jeanne into a spacious lounge.

Ruby spotted a row of Adam's books on an overflowing bookshelf and she caught him glancing at them too. She wondered if he'd mention he was the real Adam Jacobs, but decided he probably wouldn't. Not if he was trying to stay in the area incognito.

'Please take a seat,' said Jeanne, 'and I'll fetch us some tea.'

'So far so good,' whispered Adam as they both sank into a brightly patterned sofa.

'Yeah,' whispered Ruby. 'I can't believe I've found out that my great-grandmother was called Ann and that I look a lot like her. Pops never mentioned his family. You'd have thought he'd have brought it up if I really do look that much like her.'

'You must be very similar for Jeanne to notice the resemblance. It was straight away and there was no doubt in her mind,' said Adam, glancing around the room.

Ruby wanted to discuss it some more but she fell silent as she heard the clink of china cups being carried in their direction. Adam leapt up as Jeanne came in burdened with a massive tray.

'Let me help,' he said, swiftly taking the tray and looking around for somewhere to place it.

'Thank you,' said Jeanne.

Adam stood holding the tray aloft as their hostess arranged small tables in strategic places. When she was satisfied, he put the tray down on the nearest table and waited while she handed out cups. When they were settled, Jeanne handed round a plate piled high with chocolate biscuits. Ruby balanced one on the edge of her saucer. She felt too nervous to eat but as the smell of chocolate hit her, she couldn't help but pick the biscuit up and take a bite. And then, because it was so delicious, she polished it off in three quick mouthfuls. Beside her Adam did the same.

'So how is Alwyn?' asked Jeanne.

'My grandfather died earlier this

year,' said Ruby simply.

'Goodness me,' said Jeanne. 'I am surprised. I always imagined Alwyn would have outlived us all. He was so fit and healthy. I don't think I ever knew him not to be involved in one sports team or another.'

Ruby nodded sadly. Pops' heart attack had taken them all by surprise. Everyone had tried to reassure Ruby and her family that it was the way he would have wanted to go; quickly and without any lingering pain or illness.

Ruby understood that people were trying to make her feel better, but she believed Pops wouldn't have wanted to go at all. Like the rest of his family he'd probably believed he had at least twenty years left to live. It was best not to think about that right now or Ruby would start to cry.

'Wherever did he go after he left prison? No, don't tell me. It's obvious, he went to America where he met a nice girl and had a family of which you're the result. Am I right?'

'Yes, that's right,' agreed Ruby.

'Of course it is. The question is then, why have you come to see me today?' asked Jeanne with her characteristic briskness.

Ruby half expected their hostess to answer her own question but it seemed this time that she couldn't guess at the answer.

'I'm here because Pops — I mean my grandfather, Alwyn — never talked about his life in Wales and my family and I wanted to know more about it.'

'Ah,' said Jeanne. 'I see. Well you didn't flinch when I mentioned the prison so you must know about that already.'

'I only found out last Saturday,' Ruby told her.

Jeanne raised an eyebrow and nibbled on the edge of her biscuit.

'We've been to see Laura Henry,' Ruby continued. 'I know she believes Pops murdered her brother Charles. We've also found out that Pops served time in prison for manslaughter. I find it very hard to believe that the man I knew all my life could be guilty of either of those things.'

Jeanne put her saucer down and brushed imaginary crumbs off her lap.

'I see,' she said. For a long moment she gazed out of her lounge window. 'My husband, Jim, is out there,' she said, lifting a hand and pointing. 'He's working on the garden. It's a real passion of his. He's a good man with a kind heart. Jim doesn't know about Charles. I don't know why I never told him that I'd loved someone before I met him. I haven't talked about Charles in so long, but my heart still aches from time to time for the boy who never got a chance to grow old.'

Out of the corner of her eye Ruby saw Adam's hand sneak towards the tray of chocolate biscuits. Despite the seriousness of the situation she had the sudden urge to giggle. Adam's hand closed around the nearest biscuit and he pulled it towards him, not once taking his eyes off Jeanne. She admired his strategy but she was too far away from the plate to attempt the same.

'Laura adored her younger brother,' continued Jeanne. 'As did I. I was quite mad with grief when he died and, like Laura, I blamed Alwyn. When Laura kicked up a fuss saying that Alwyn had killed Charles, I supported her. I provided evidence at his trial that they were arguing a lot before that horrible boat trip. I agreed with her that Alwyn was jealous of Charles. Afterwards, when I'd heard that Alwyn had disappeared, I tried to put the whole thing out of mind.'

Jeanne picked up her tea cup and took a sip.

'Do you have children?' she asked Ruby.

'No,' answered Ruby, taken aback.

'Don't leave it too late,' said Jeanne. 'Women do these days, and then they find they can't have them because they're too old. Having a child is the best, most rewarding thing you can do but it's very tiring. No one can really tell you what it's like to get up in the middle of the night to feed your baby. It's as if you've been stranded on a dark island with no one around you for miles. You feel totally alone. I suppose it might be different now, what with smart phones and on-demand TV, but in the 1970s there was nothing. Nothing to distract you from your thoughts.'

Ruby glanced at Adam who was frowning, obviously wondering, like herself, where this monologue was going. He turned to look at her and whatever he saw in her expression caused him to reach across and link his fingers with hers.

'Alone in those dark hours, which stretched on and on, I thought about Alwyn and Charles a lot and my convictions began to crumble. Laura's belief that Alwyn was in love with me was absurd. I think I knew that even when Charles' death was still fresh, but I was so angry and I wanted there to be a reason for his death. But in those still, calm hours of the night when it was only me and baby Liam, I examined every facet of that summer and I came to doubt my convictions.'

Jeanne paused to take a sip of tea.

'Alwyn never gave any indication that he liked me any more than as a friend. There was not one single look, touch or word spoken to suggest that he had feelings for me. As for Alwyn being jealous of Charles because of his education, I came not to believe that either. Alwyn was a popular pupil at the local school. He was a big fish in a small pond. He wouldn't have wanted to leave.'

'So what do you think happened?' asked Ruby.

Jeanne fiddled with the hem of her cardigan. She took a deep breath and looked Ruby squarely in the eyes.

'It is true that they were arguing a lot over that summer. Now that Alwyn's dead I guess we'll never know what it was about. It's my belief that they argued again on that dreadful day. I think they got into a fight that turned physical. Alwyn was so much stronger than Charles. I don't think he intended to seriously hurt him but one punch would easily have been enough to send Charles overboard. It wasn't a big boat. Charles must have been knocked unconscious in the process and drowned before Alwyn could pull him out.'

'But Pops would never hurt anyone!' Ruby cried out.

Adam's fingers tightened on hers and she clung to him. Could Pops really have punched someone? It didn't seem possible to her at all.

Jeanne put her cup and saucer down on the table in front of her.

'Perhaps his time in jail changed him,' Jeanne suggested. 'Maybe he learned to curb his temper. I doubt it was pleasant and I would imagine he never wanted to go back.'

Ruby opened her mouth to protest but Jeanne silenced her with a raised hand.

'The truth of the matter is that two boys went sailing off and only one came back. Something awful definitely happened, because no one saw Charles alive again. I can't remember what Alwyn said in his defence but it was something along the lines of him not knowing what had happened to Charles. It was a very weak explanation and even the court agreed, which was why he was found guilty of manslaughter. I know that's not what you want to hear, but it is the truth.'

Ruby felt Adam flinch and she realised she was gripping his hand so tightly her knuckles had turned white. She released his hand and looped her fingers through her cup handle.

'Thank you for telling us your side of the story,' she said, in a low, calm voice she didn't recognise as her own.

Jeanne nodded tightly and turned to the window.

'Jim's coming back inside,' she said, 'so I'd be grateful if we could change the subject.'

'Of course,' said Ruby in her new calm voice.

'I see you're into crime fiction,' said Adam, taking control of the conversation.

Ruby leaned back in her seat and sipped on her tea as Adam took Jeanne through her favourite authors. Preferring books on legends, Ruby had no idea what they were talking about. She wouldn't have been able to contribute anyway. Not with her mind so full of Pops. Could he really have done such a thing? Could he have punched someone so hard he knocked them unconscious?

Ruby remembered a hot, sticky afternoon when she'd been six. Pops had caught her filling a bucket with stones.

'What are you doing, little one?' he'd asked.

'Stevie was mean to me,' she'd replied, referring to her seven-year-old neighbour and nemesis.

'OK,' Pops had said, crouching down so he was on a level with her. 'So what're you gonna do with those stones?'

'Throw them at him,' she'd stated simply.

'I see,' Pops had said. Then he'd very

slowly prised the bucket from her hands. Using very gentle fingers he'd turned her face until she was looking into his eyes. 'Violence solves nothing,' he'd said kindly but firmly. 'Let's imagine that you throw these stones at Stevie. That will make him mad so he may throw something back at you. You'll both get hurt. Then your mom and dad will argue with his mom and dad and the whole thing will get out of hand. Instead of throwing stones at him why don't we invite him to come and make some ice cream with us?'

For the rest of the summer Ruby and Stevie had played together. In her memory, Pops was always in the background keeping a watchful eye on them. Pops had talked her out of making an enemy, and her nemesis had become her friend. She'd cried when Stevie and his family had moved to California the following fall.

Her childhood memory was full of scenes like that where Pops had been the voice of reason when any family member had become cross. Had he been like that from birth, or had his experiences changed him? It was looking likely that they would never find out.

Ruby jolted when Adam nudged her leg and she realised he was winding down the conversation.

'Thank you so much for your time,' she said, when a gap in the chat presented itself.

'That was my pleasure,' said Jeanne, looking suitably flushed.

Adam had obviously turned on the charm while Ruby had been lost in her past.

'Thank you for the lovely biscuits as well,' said Ruby, standing and smoothing her dress.

'You must take some with you,' said Jeanne. 'I'll put some in some foil.'

Jeanne disappeared with the plate. At least some good was going to come out of this morning. Ruby loved those biscuits.

'How are you doing?' murmured Adam, as they made their way to the front door.

'I'm all right,' said Ruby.

The hallway was quiet apart from the faint murmur of voices coming from deeper inside the bungalow. They stood by their shoes and Ruby resisted the urge to lean into Adam and rest her head on his chest.

'Here you go,' said Jeanne, reappearing with the biscuits tightly wrapped in foil and put in a clear plastic bag.

'Thank you,' said Ruby warmly, taking the bag and then slipping on her sandals.

'When you next see Dylan, give him my best,' said Jeanne.

Ruby froze. Who was Dylan?

'Who?' said Adam for her.

'Dylan,' repeated Jeanne. She looked at Ruby, then Adam and then back again. 'Dylan Turner, Alwyn's younger brother.'

12

Adam hadn't written anything for two days what with his longer-than-planned trip to Bristol and going with Ruby to meet Jeanne. His latest manuscript deadline was looming, and earlier today he'd read an email from his publicist asking him for four days of his time next week to promote his latest novel being released in paperback.

He should be writing like a demon because if he didn't hit his word target by this Friday, he was going to be delivering his manuscript late. He'd never been late before. He'd even managed to deliver a manuscript on time two weeks after Clara left him.

His fingers were resting on top of his keyboard. On screen, the cursor blinked at him. He knew what he wanted to say and how he wanted to say it but he couldn't make his fingers move.

He kept seeing Ruby's face after their visit to Jeanne's bungalow yesterday. She'd looked punch-drunk from all the revelations, and he couldn't blame her. It must have been such a shock to find out that her grandfather had a brother he'd never spoken of.

Jeanne hadn't known where Dylan lived now. After Alwyn had been sent to prison, the family had moved away, never to be seen in Carwyn Bay again. She had heard that they'd stayed in Wales but she couldn't be more specific than that and she couldn't be sure that it was even true or whether it was local gossip. The family could have easily moved somewhere as far away as Australia — in which case they'd probably never find Dylan.

On the drive back to Melveryn Manor, Adam and Ruby had discussed the best ways to find him. They'd come up with two strategies, both of which were pretty basic. Ruby would search for any references to a Dylan Turner who would be in his early sixties, and

Adam would phone Nick to see whether he would help.

Adam had left a message on Nick's voicemail but hadn't had a reply. If Nick was busy on a case Adam wouldn't normally hear back from him until it was over — but if Nick was still in an accommodating mood, then he might prioritise Adam's request. There was no way of knowing.

Adam pushed back his chair and stood up. Maybe if he went to see whether Ruby was OK, he could get her out of his head and concentrate on his work instead.

It shouldn't matter that he was wearing track suit bottoms, but it did. Annoyed with himself for caring about how he looked, he went into his bedroom and changed into jeans. He glanced into the mirror, telling himself that it was just to check that he didn't have any ink smudges on his face, but he tweaked his hair nonetheless.

He strode down the corridor that connected the two parts of the house and pulled open the connecting door. He wasn't expecting Ruby to be on the other side of it. Her arm raised to knock, she overbalanced and fell at his feet.

'Are you OK?' asked Adam, trying and failing to control his laughter as he bent to help her up.

'I'm good,' she said, accepting his hand. She giggled as he pulled her to her feet. 'At least we've both done that now.'

'Thanks for reminding me of the embarrassing time we met,' said Adam, keeping hold of her hand even though she was now standing.

Ruby grinned mischievously at him. She was so close he could see flecks of gold in her irises.

'You don't have to knock next time, just come on through,' said Adam, realising that he never knocked when he went to see her.

She smiled up at him and for a moment Adam forgot all his reasons for not wanting a relationship with Ruby.

Was he out of his mind for denying himself?

'I have news,' she announced, snapping him back to reality.

'You've found Dylan Turner,' Adam guessed.

'No, it's not that exciting. Well, maybe it has the potential to be. Estelle's just been over and she's given me the key to the mystery room.'

Grinning triumphantly, she held up a silver key.

'Want to see what's inside?' she asked.

'I'd love to,' said Adam.

Ruby's good mood was infectious. Reluctantly he let go of her hand and followed her through the house.

'Were you coming to see me?' she asked.

'I was. I wanted to let you know that I'd left a message with Nick but haven't had a response yet.'

It was a weak excuse but Ruby didn't seem to notice.

'I've not had much luck either,' she

confided. 'I searched online and tried different permutations of Dylan Turner and Wales. I had over thirty different hits but none of them took me anywhere that seemed even remotely close to my family. That got me thinking that even if his parents may have stayed in Wales, it doesn't follow that he did. Maybe he moved to England for work, or anywhere in the entire world. I tried searching for Dylan Turner and England, and came up with over a hundred hits. I was going through the names and trying to sort them into 'definitely not' and 'possible' when Estelle arrived with the key.'

'Where did she get the key?' asked Adam.

'Apparently Laura likes us. When Estelle contacted her to see if she knew anything about the locked door, she was very complimentary about our visit. It turns out we're the only people who've ever worked here to bother to go and see her and she wanted us to see inside the room. We're under strict instructions not to disturb anything. Obviously I feel guilty about her trust in us because our visit had an ulterior motive, but I've promised myself I'll go and visit her again. I'll take some rose cuttings from the garden she loves so much.'

'Did Estelle tell you what to expect in the room?'

'Yes!' gasped Ruby. 'I can't believe I haven't told you that bit already. It's Charles' old bedroom.' Ruby stopped a few yards from the door and gripped Adam's arm. 'Can you imagine what's in there? We could be finding out what Charles and Pops were arguing about that summer within the next ten minutes.'

Adam looked down at Ruby. Her skin was flushed, her curly hair flying out in every direction. He wanted to smooth the curls away from her face and run his thumb along her jaw.

'What if you just find a typical teenage boy's room? Covered in posters of women?'

Ruby frowned. 'Did they have posters like that in the 1950s?'

Adam shrugged. 'The 1950s equivalent. I doubt teenage boys have changed much over the years.'

Ruby laughed and Adam realised that was becoming one of his favourite sounds. He moved his arm away from her as he clung to the strands of his resolve to keep whatever was between them as a friendship only.

'Shall we?' he asked, nodding at the door.

Ruby cleared her throat, slid the key into the lock and turned it slowly. She stopped and looked up at Adam.

'Here goes,' she said and pushed the door.

For a long moment they both stood on the threshold and looked inside. Adam had been wrong; there were no pictures of half-clad women on any of the walls. A wooden bed frame stood at one end of the room with blankets still covering it. A matching side table, stacked with books, was placed next to it. On another wall was a large writing desk with a tall book shelf on its right. In front of a wardrobe a pair of shoes lay abandoned as if they had been kicked off moments before.

'Oh, this is really sad,' whispered Ruby. 'It's as if Charles has popped out for a few minutes and is going to come back in any second now.'

Adam nodded. The room did have the feeling as if its owner had only just left.

Ruby made her way over to the writing desk, covered in sheaves of paper, neatly stacked.

'It seems a shame to touch anything,' she said soberly.

'I'm surprised Laura gave us the key,' said Adam, stepping into the room and turning in a circle. 'It seems way too private.'

'I agree,' said Ruby, who was picking up the topmost piece of paper and reading through it. 'I wonder what she thought we would do with it.'

'Did Estelle say you could open the

room up to the public?' asked Adam.

'No, Estelle said Laura was emphatically against anyone else other than you and I seeing inside. Apparently we seem trustworthy.' Ruby pulled a face. 'Obviously we aren't, though.'

She put the piece of paper back down.

'What did that say?' asked Adam.

'It's instructions on how to dissect a frog,' said Ruby, smiling. 'It looks like an essay. Maybe he was studying biology at university or a similar subject. I'm guessing that if anything relevant to his death was on this table, Laura or her parents would have found it and used it in the trial against Pops.'

'Should we search the room?' asked Adam, keen to do so but not wanting to overstep the mark. This was not his problem to solve after all.

'I think we should do it methodically,' said Ruby, moving further into the room. 'We'll have to photograph everything before we move it so we can put it back exactly how it was.'

Adam nodded, although he doubted anyone would notice if a few things were out of place. The room hadn't been opened in years, and it was unlikely that Laura Henry would ever be well enough to come back and see it.

'Let's start with the papers on the desk,' said Ruby. She pulled out her phone and snapped pictures of the desk from different angles. She took a small pile of papers for herself and handed another to Adam.

They settled with their backs against the wooden bed frame. Adam slid the first piece of paper from the top of his pile. Charles' writing was neatly elegant and Adam admired his sentence structure. For a serious essay, Charles knew how to engage his reader so that even quite a dry subject was interesting.

'Hmm,' murmured Ruby after a few minutes of silence. 'This isn't looking promising. All I seem to have is a lot of scholarly work. How about you?'

Adam sneezed and rubbed his nose. 'I've got a lot of essays too and . . . ' He sneezed again. 'Several years of dust.'

'Oh, sorry, I gave you paper from the top of the pile,' said Ruby guiltily.

Adam sneezed again.

'I think,' he said, 'we're going to have to skim read a lot of this or we'll be here for hours. We'll learn quite a lot about the internal workings of various animals but I'm not sure that's useful.'

Ruby put her pile of paper down and rubbed her face.

'Are you all right?' he asked.

'I'm fine,' she said, dropping her hands away from her head. She looked at Adam. 'This is going to sound naïve but I wasn't expecting this search to be so hard. I thought I'd come over to the UK and find that Pops had had some silly falling-out over a girl or that he'd argued with his parents about his choice of career. I wasn't expecting murder charges and it never crossed my mind that he might have ended up in prison. What if we wade through all this and never find out what really happened? Or worse, what if Pops really did kill someone? I'll love him whatever the answer, and so will the rest of my family, but it will still be devastating.'

Adam slung his arm around Ruby and pulled her close to him. She didn't resist and as she drew close she rested her head on his chest. He lifted his hand and stroked her curls.

He didn't know what to say to her. Yes, everything she had found out was sad for her family — but he could never regret any of it because it had led her to him, and he was increasingly finding that he didn't want their time together to end.

13

Ruby tugged Charles' bed away from the wall and slowly pushed it across the bedroom floor. She was very careful not to nudge the shoes Charles had discarded outside his wardrobe.

It was possible the shoes had been dumped there after his death, but she felt that they were exactly how he had left them when he had last gone from the room. Ruby wanted to honour his last movements, especially as she was going through his private things so relentlessly.

In the eight days since she'd been given the key to the room, she'd been through every piece of paper she could find. She'd searched through drawers and cupboards and even in the pockets of clothes for anything that could shed light on Charles' untimely death. She'd felt guilty going through his personal effects, but she figured that even if she found even a tiny shred of evidence to suggest Pops was innocent of killing Charles, then it was worth it.

There was nothing under Charles' bed except for dust.

Ruby swept a brush over the newly exposed floor and then crouched down. She was glad no one was around to see her as she ran her fingers around the edges of the room searching for a place where the floorboards were loose. Finding nothing, she pressed around the exposed floor feeling for hidden compartments, knowing how crazy she seemed. She didn't even know what she was searching for. What could Charles have possibly hidden that would shed light on his death? But to have come this far and not bother to search thoroughly would be a waste, so she was looking into every nook and cranny she could find.

She rocked back onto her heels and knelt looking at the floor. The wooden flooring looked very secure around the edges and she hadn't felt anything out of place underneath. There were no hidden compartments here.

She glanced at her watch. It was getting late and she'd wanted an early night to get ready for tomorrow. She was going on her date with Adam! Although she wasn't sure if he thought their planned day out was a date or not. She'd not seen him much in the last eight days, although she'd been counting down the hours until she could spend an entire day with him. He'd been writing frantically and she'd been either searching this room or preparing food for the café. She'd made another couple of lemon drizzle cakes, still without success.

She'd served customers for a whole weekend and not batted an eyelid, not even when the tiny café had every chair filled. All she'd been able to think about was getting back to Charles' bedroom and searching some more.

Now there was only really one place left to search and that was underneath the desk. She glanced at her watch again. Did she have enough time to move everything off the desk and arrange it in such a way that she could easily put everything back in the right place? She'd need to take out the drawers as well, because it was solid wood and not easy to move. She'd already tilted it forward to see whether anything had dropped behind, but nothing had. Was it worth the effort?

She needed to make sure her outfit was dry for tomorrow. Adam had kept his plans a secret, but had told her that she needed to be in clothes she was comfortable walking in and that she'd need to bring a picnic. She'd offered to make one for him too, and he'd accepted gratefully.

The picnic was ready. She'd made baguettes with thick slices of ham and generous portions of a caramelised chutney she'd discovered the other day in a shop in the village, and to which she was quickly becoming addicted. She'd picked some strawberries she'd found growing rampantly in the wild, and added slices of a variety of cakes. They would eat like kings — but she was not having as much luck with her outfit.

She'd decided to wear jeans with a simple, short-sleeved red blouse. She'd given it a wash earlier to freshen it up and had hung it in the sun to dry, where it had been caught in a summer shower. Now, instead of looking fresh her favourite blouse was looking like a crumbled tablecloth. It was now drying in her bathroom.

She really should go and check on it because she didn't want to wear anything else tomorrow. All her other outfits had felt wrong somehow. The blouse was the perfect combination of smart and casual.

Instead of heading back down to her room, however, she started to take piles of paper off the desk. She'd only be burning with curiosity if she didn't move the desk tonight. Thinking about what she might find underneath it might spoil her day tomorrow and she wanted it to be perfect.

Even if Adam was only interested in spending the day with her as a friend, then she still wanted to give him her undivided attention. He said he'd come to terms with his best friend marrying his ex-fiancée, but he had to be feeling a little upset. She wanted to give him a good day out and to keep him distracted and focused solely on her. She wouldn't be able to do that if part of her was still in this room thinking that maybe, just maybe, there was something hidden underneath the desk.

She pulled the drawers of the desk out and checked for hidden compartments. There weren't any, but she already knew that because she'd looked before.

She tugged at the desk, but even without the drawers it was still heavy and difficult to move. She budged it an inch but then it stuck fast. She straightened up and looked at it. She moved it enough so that she could just about fit her leg between the back of the desk and the wall. Feeling that pushing was better than pulling, she wedged her leg in the space and gave the desk a shove.

The desk moved a little and she stood up panting with effort. She wasn't going to get the desk back into position easily. Hopefully Adam would help her move it back after their day out tomorrow.

She took a deep breath and pushed again. This time the desk moved forward a couple of inches and as it did so, something heavy landed on her foot.

'Fiddlesticks!' she shouted out as pain shot up her leg. She couldn't swear, even though Mom and Grams were over five thousand miles away. They'd ingrained the message that swearing was bad from a very early age and to the amusement of her colleagues she couldn't break the habit, even in extreme circumstances.

She pulled her leg out from behind the desk and held her foot up for inspection. The skin was red and angry-looking, but not cut and it didn't appear to be swelling up. She hadn't broken anything and the pain was already subsiding.

She glanced down behind the desk to see what had fallen, hoping it wasn't an integral part that had broken off. She didn't know how she would explain to Estelle or Laura how that had happened.

The object appeared to be large and silver-coloured, which meant it couldn't be part of the oak desk. She leaned down and pulled it out, needing two hands because of its weight.

She discovered she was holding a rectangular, tin box around A4 size; it was dented on one side and on the other was a handle. The handle was fitted with a small, black padlock.

Ruby put the box down and felt behind the desk. There she could feel a ledge where the box must have been sitting all this time. She ran her fingers all around the gap caused by the ledge but there was no key. She tried the other side of the desk, but if a key had ever been there, it definitely wasn't now. She'd searched the rest of the room and knew there were no keys to be found anywhere.

She sat back down and picked the box up. She traced the seam that ran all the way around the box, looking for a weak point but she didn't find one. She tugged on the padlock but it didn't budge.

She got slowly to her feet, holding the box to her chest as she did so.

Tomorrow she would show Adam what she'd found, and hopefully he could help her open the box. Whatever happened, she was going to get it to reveal its secrets. This surely had to be a vital clue — not bank statements or something equally dull!

14

Ruby sprang out of bed and checked her clock. It was only a few minutes after six in the morning. How was that possible? She'd been lying awake for what seemed like hours waiting for the day to begin. She wasn't due to meet Adam for another four hours. How was she going to pass the time between now and then? She couldn't spend another second in bed.

It was way too early to get dressed and put make-up on; she'd only need to do it again before they met up.

Instead she pulled a cardigan on over her nightie, slipped into a pair of flip flops and headed up to the café. She could make herself breakfast in her room but the café, with its view of the sea, was a much pleasanter prospect.

She took her time assembling a breakfast of creamy yogurt, topped with berries and crunchy granola. When she was done she unlocked the café door and stepped out onto the terrace. The sun was already warming the tables and burning off yesterday's showers. Ruby popped her glass of juice down on a table top and slid into a seat. Holding her bowl in one hand and a spoon in the other she gazed out to sea. In the distance a large tanker sat, seemingly unmoving. Closer to the shore a sailing boat bobbed along at a rapid pace. Ruby watched it until it sailed out of sight.

The café was prepared and ready for tomorrow, with cakes stored in the freezer to be removed when she got back this evening. She'd made large vats of soup and chilli and frozen them in individual portions. There was nothing she had to do this morning. She could pass her spare time prepping for her teaching modules next term, but she didn't fancy that. The weather was too lovely to be cooped up inside working on her laptop.

Instead she went back inside and pulled on an old pair of shorts, a baggy T-shirt and trainers. She'd worked out two possible coves in which the ill-fated picnic may have taken place and she'd been meaning to check them out. Now was as good a time as any.

She set out at a gentle jog. She hadn't done much running since staying in Wales and it wasn't long before her legs began to feel the burn. She welcomed the feeling; it made her feel alive. She ran along a path that ran along the cliff edge, stopping every now and then to look down for any obvious stretches of sand.

After forty minutes she turned round and headed for home. She'd seen a couple of potential sites but they had been inaccessible from the land. This did fit with the description of the cove given by Laura, and so either of them could be the right place, but it was still very frustrating. Ruby had no idea how she would get access to a boat — and even if she could, what would the excursion tell her really?

Ruby let herself back into the house and stopped only to drink a large glass of water before quickly heading to the bathroom. She took a long, relaxing shower, letting the warm spray soothe her muscles. The run had burned off some of her nervous energy and once she'd dried her hair into some semblance of control she was feeling a lot calmer. She decided it was going to be too hot a day for jeans and she pulled on a denim skirt instead. The red blouse was looking a lot better for being dry and ironed and she pulled that on too. She leaned down so she could see her face in the tiny mirror and applied her make-up, taking considerable care not to look as if she had taken any care at all.

She glanced at the clock. Finally it was time to meet Adam.

She grabbed her handbag and the tin box she'd found last night and headed round to the front of the house where they'd agreed to meet. He was already there, leaning against the hood of his car, arms folded and watching her approach. Her knees wobbled slightly as their eyes met and his mouth broke into a broad grin.

'Hey,' he said as she got nearer. 'What's with the box?'

'I found it,' said Ruby, passing the box to him, 'in Charles' room. It was hidden behind his desk.'

'Did you open it?' he asked.

'No.' Ruby pointed to the padlock. 'Because of that.'

'Huh.'

Adam put the box down on the gravelled driveway and turned it so that it was on its side. He grabbed the box with one hand and the padlock in the other and gave the lock a hard tug. It snapped off with a crunching noise.

'Oh! That's one way to do it, I suppose.'

Adam grinned up at her. 'Don't be disappointed if this is where you find his stash of posters,' he said, handing the box to Ruby.

'Are you on about the scantily-clad women again?' Ruby asked with a raised eyebrow.

Adam laughed. 'I'm just telling you how boys operate.'

Ruby raised an eyebrow.

'Some boys,' Adam clarified. 'Obviously I'm an exception. Only contemporary art lined my bedroom walls as I grew up.'

Ruby snorted.

'Shall we sit in the car to open the box?' said Adam. 'We don't want to risk a sea breeze whipping up and spiriting away whatever's inside.'

'Good idea,' said Ruby, thanking Adam as he opened the passenger door for her.

She waited until Adam had climbed into the driver's seat before gently prising the box open. Inside were sheaves of yellowing paper. Ruby picked up the first piece of paper and started to read.

'What is it?' asked Adam, after a few minutes of silence.

'It's poetry,' whispered Ruby. 'Really

beautiful poetry.'

She handed the sheet to Adam and then picked up the next one.

They read in silence for a while, handing pieces of paper between them when they read a piece they thought the other would enjoy.

'He was very talented,' said Adam eventually.

'Yes,' said Ruby, putting the paper she was reading down. 'He really was. What a tragedy that he died so young and didn't get to show the world he was every bit as much a genius as his famous forebear.'

'We should give these to his sister,' said Adam.

'Yes,' said Ruby, as she gently slid the pieces of paper back into the box.

'We'll be passing near her home later on today. We could drop them off then,' suggested Adam.

'Let's do that,' said Ruby, pleased that she would be able to bring some joy to the frail lady. This was obviously the writing Laura and her parents had hunted for after Charles' death and which they hadn't found. Why had Charles hidden it? Yet another mystery they probably would never find out the answer to.

'For now,' said Ruby, 'I'll put this box in your boot and then we can set off on this mysterious day. I'm really intrigued as to where you're going to take me. It's not going to be scary, is it?'

Adam grinned. 'You'll have to wait and see.'

'Are you going to give me any sort of clue?' asked Ruby, as Adam pulled off the driveway and headed away from the manor.

'We're going for a walk,' said Adam.

'A long one?' Ruby asked. She hoped so. She wanted to spend as long as possible with Adam.

'It can be as long or as short as you like but I think you're going to want to keep walking when you see where we're headed.'

'Ooh, I'm really intrigued.'

Adam smiled again. Ruby was

pleased to see it. So far his mood seemed to be very upbeat. He didn't seem to be dwelling on what his best friend and ex-fiancée were up to today.

She settled back into the seat and relaxed into the comfortable quietness. She was glad she'd relaxed enough around Adam now that she didn't feel the need to fill the silence with conversation. Every now and then she glanced at him to check he wasn't frowning or looking tense. After a while she sensed he was fighting laughter.

'What is it?' she said, when his mouth curved into a wide grin.

'You.' He chortled. 'You don't have to keep checking on me. I'm not about to burst into tears.'

'Maybe I was just checking out the view from your window,' retorted Ruby, feeling heat rush across her cheeks. She'd really thought that she was being discreet — but had obviously failed.

'We're nearly there,' he said. 'Keep an eye out for the Pendragon Pub. That's where we'll park.'

A few minutes later he pulled into a large car park that was already filling with customers.

'Are you going to tell me where we're going?' asked Ruby as he turned into a tight space.

'This whole area,' said Adam, unclipping his seat belt, 'is strongly associated with King Arthur. There are several walking trails here or we can do a big loop and take in all the sights.'

Ruby couldn't answer for a moment. She hadn't expected to spend the day doing something she was interested in. She'd been fully prepared to go to some gruesome museum looking at artefacts from famous crimes. Previous boyfriends would have done just that. Not that Adam was a boyfriend, unfortunately.

'Let's do the long walk that takes in all the sights,' she said eventually with a radiant grin.

★ ★ ★

The early parts of the path were paved and packed densely with people. As they continued to walk, both the people and the paving gradually disappeared. Eventually it was only the two of them on a dried mud path with just enough space for them to walk side by side, their shoulders and hands occasionally bumping together.

Adam held a guidebook and pointed out significant features as they walked along. At one point they passed a large standing stone said to be a pebble Arthur had found in his shoe. According to the legend he'd taken it out and thrown it from the neighbouring county. On its journey to its final resting place it had grown in size until it had become this giant boulder in front of them. Another stone was meant to show a horse print from Arthur's own horse but whichever way they squinted at it Ruby and Adam couldn't see anything that even slightly resembled a print.

After a couple of hours of walking

they stopped for lunch near a small stone circle. The circle had no claims to Arthur but it did have a view of a nearby river and a comfortable-looking slope covered in springy grass. Adam spread a blanket and Ruby covered it in picnic food.

'Any luck finding Dylan Turner?' asked Adam, as they munched on their ham baguettes.

'None at all. I'm guessing there's no word from Nick?'

'I heard from him yesterday but it was to say that he hasn't had time to look. He promised to prioritise it after his honeymoon.'

Ruby pulled a face. 'Sorry I brought that up.'

'Honestly, Ruby, I'm not upset. You don't need to tiptoe around my feelings,' Adam assured her.

'You must be feeling a bit weird about it.'

Adam tilted his head to one side and munched on his sandwich. After a while he said, 'If they hadn't got together I would be married to Clara by now and that would have been a disaster.'

'Why's that?' asked Ruby, curiosity getting the better of her resolve not to bring up the topic of Clara or Nick today.

Adam leaned back onto his elbow and stretched out his legs. Ruby copied him so that they were lying facing each other. Adam started to pick at the strawberries.

'Clara is lovely,' said Adam. 'She's a kind and gentle person, who loves the company of others.'

Ruby felt a lurch of jealousy as she waited for the 'but' she hoped was coming.

'The problem was,' Adam continued, 'that I spend a lot of time researching and writing my books, which is a solitary occupation. When I'm not doing that, I'm involved in an intensive promotion programme, which often involves being away from home for weeks at a time. Clara was alone a lot, which was an almost permanent source of guilt for me. She and I were growing apart when we decided to go on a summer holiday with Nick and his then girlfriend.'

This wasn't the character assassination Ruby was hoping for. She'd been hoping Adam would open up about how horrible Clara had been as a girlfriend, but she was left feeling sorry for her.

Ruby flipped open the container filled with brownies and picked one from the top. Its soft, chocolatey texture helped her feel better.

'Days before the holiday, Nick's girlfriend decided not to come. I think their relationship had come to a natural end but I didn't know that at the time.' Adam continued as he helped himself to some brownies too. 'I spent most of the holiday indoors writing, so Nick and Clara were thrown together.

'She tried to get me to join them but I was in sight of a deadline and I kept fobbing them both off. At the end of the holiday Clara told me it was over between us and I wasn't that upset.

'A few weeks later they came to the flat I'd moved into to tell me they'd started a relationship. They looked stricken with guilt. I said some things I really regret and asked them to leave. I know that they didn't set out to hurt me and I still feel awful about what I said to them. It doesn't seem to have completely destroyed my relationship with Nick, though, for which I am incredibly grateful.'

Ruby took another brownie and mulled over what Adam had just said. Although he'd said nothing against Clara, he hadn't sung her praises either. He didn't sound like a heartbroken man and there was one big factor that sprang out at her. He had a deadline in sight right now — and yet he wasn't chained to his computer. He'd been helping her in the kitchen and with her quest to find out about Pops, and now here he was with her, lying on a picnic rug and basking in the summer sun.

There was no way today could be

classed as research for a new book, so what was going on? She was about to make a huge leap of faith. She hoped it paid off.

'Also,' said Ruby, 'if you had stayed with her then you wouldn't be here with me.'

Adam's gaze flicked up from the picnic blanket and met hers.

He cleared his throat. 'Indeed.'

Ruby grinned at him and the corners of his lips twitched. She leaned over and gently pressed her lips against his. Then she leaned back and looked at him.

He didn't move. They stared at each other for a long moment. She moved to kiss him again but this time his arm came up between them and he held her at a distance.

'Ruby . . . ' he whispered. 'You're so lovely but this is a bad idea.'

'Why?' asked Ruby, dread and embarrassment curling together in her stomach.

'I'm so much older than you.'

Ruby let out a burst of relieved laughter.

'Is that all you're worried about? Nine years is nothing. There's ten years between my parents and you'd never know.'

Her confidence returning, Ruby leaned forward and kissed Adam again. For a few delicious seconds he kissed her back before breaking away again.

'I mean it, Ruby. I'm too old for you — and I don't mean in just age,' he said firmly.

'What do you mean by that?' asked Ruby, baffled.

'I'm . . . well, actually no, let's start with you. You're so beautiful and vibrant. You're like an exotic bird. If you were with me I'd start to clip your wings in the same way I did to Clara. Your vivacity would start to fade. I would hate for that to happen.'

Ruby reached over and stroked his jaw. Adam turned to her touch despite himself.

'No one's ever described me so

beautifully before,' she said.

Her fingers trailed down to his shoulder and Adam inhaled sharply. There was no denying he was attracted to her. As they'd been talking, their bodies had moved closer and there was now only a hair's breadth between them.

'I think this has more to do with your relationship with Clara than with us,' she said. 'You think that any woman is going to leave you like she did because you're so devoted to your work. But I'm not her. I know your work is important to you and I would never expect you around to entertain me all the time. I'm a grown woman. I can entertain myself.'

'There's also the matter of you living in the States,' said Adam, leaning down and brushing his lips against her forehead. 'Whatever happens between us now will begin with the ending already in sight.'

'Stop worrying so much,' said Ruby, sliding her hand across the mat and threading her fingers with his. 'We're here now. Let's enjoy ourselves and live for the moment.'

Ruby knew she had won the argument when Adam's free hand came up to cup her face and he brought his mouth down to hers.

15

The late afternoon sun warmed the car as Adam zipped along the country lanes. Ruby felt happiness fizzing inside her.

She snuck a glance at Adam. A smile was playing at the corner of his mouth. He must have felt her gaze because, without taking his eyes off the road, he reached across and threaded his fingers with hers. She pulled their clasped hands onto her lap and studied his hand, which was so different from hers. His long fingers curled around hers and she traced the blue veins on the back of his hand with her fingertips.

Today had been perfect. The walk in the sunshine, the kissing on the picnic rug, the leisurely stroll afterwards and now the shared joy bouncing between them. It had been one of the happiest days of Ruby's life. No other relationship she had ever been in had started with such joyfulness.

His words about the end already being in sight bobbed to the forefront of her mind, but she pushed the thought away. If their relationship was meant to be, then they would make it work. If it was only to be these few short weeks of summer then she would relax and enjoy them to the full.

'Have you thought how you are going to present the poems to Laura?' asked Adam, taking his hand back to change gear.

'What do you mean?' asked Ruby, missing the warmth of his touch already.

'You were under strict instructions not to touch anything in the room but you obviously have, otherwise you wouldn't have found the box,' Adam pointed out.

Ruby nodded. 'I was kind of hoping she would be so pleased to have the writing restored to her that we could brush over the part where I was moving furniture around.'

Adam grinned. 'OK, well it's done

now anyway so if she's cross then I guess you'll have to brazen your way through. I'm sure you'll manage.'

Ruby mulled it over for a moment. 'I'll confess to doing a bit of gentle sweeping to get rid of the years of accumulated dust. I'll say I was careful not to disturb anything and to return furniture to its original place, which is all true. It fell down when I was cleaning around the desk and I investigated because I was worried I'd broken something, which is kind of true. KISS, remember!'

He laughed. 'I'm sure it will be fine. As you say she'd going to be thrilled to have this part of her brother returned to her. I could even suggest she has the poems published. I'm sure the Maurice Henry Trust could arrange something like that. It would be fantastic publicity for the place.'

'Yeah, good idea — just make sure it happens after I finish working there. I couldn't cope with any more visitors.'

'Has it really been that bad?' asked Adam, a frown creasing his forehead.

'It's been great fun,' Ruby reassured him. 'It's been crazy busy but it's been worth it. I've met so many lovely people and I've learned to cook. I'm mostly amazing at that now, by the way.'

Adam laughed. 'And modest too!'

'Seriously, I've loved working there far more than I thought I would. In the beginning the café and the house were afterthoughts in my quest to find out what happened to Pops, but the experience has been so different from my normal job and it's taught me so much.'

'Such as?'

'It's taught me how to bake awesome cakes. It's taught me that organisation is key to successful food preparation but it's also taught me that people who work in the food industry don't get paid nearly enough. The next time I eat out, my tip is going to be outrageous in its extravagance.'

'But you don't want any more guests because . . . ?'

'I'm run off my feet already. Every

day I open the café I make a change that makes the next time slightly easier, but as the weeks are going by I'm getting more customers. A couple of times the room has been full to capacity and I've had people waiting out in the gardens for tables to come free,' Ruby told him happily.

'I think you should get Estelle to hire someone to help you. There must be a couple of kids in the village looking for work,' Adam suggested.

'I'll ask,' said Ruby, thinking that perhaps he was right. If the café got any busier she wouldn't be able to cope, and the cakes were selling so well it was making a tidy profit.

'I expect word of your excellent cake making ability has spread and people are coming to taste the delights for themselves,' Adam teased.

'I expect you're right,' Ruby grinned. 'Do you remember my Victoria sponges in the beginning?'

They both laughed.

'We're here.' Adam turned the

purring car smoothly into the care home's long driveway.

'Already?' asked Ruby. Her joy at spending the drive chatting to Adam had made the journey whip by at speed. She was suddenly nervous about seeing Laura. What if she was really cross about how the poems were found? But not to show them to the poet's sister would be worse.

Adam opened the boot and pulled out the black box as Ruby let herself out of the car.

'I'm nervous,' she confessed.

'Don't be,' said Adam, folding her hand into his. 'I'm here with you.'

Feeling bolstered by his support and loving the feel of his skin against hers, Ruby felt much better.

* * *

They were greeted at the entrance by Sian, the nurse who had met them the first time.

'Hello again,' she said cheerfully.

'Have you come to visit Laura?'

When they confirmed that they had Sian said, 'That's so lovely. She was talking about your visit for days afterwards. She's got someone with her at the moment but I don't think he'll be much longer. Would you like to take a seat in the lounge and I'll bring you some tea?'

'That's very kind of you,' said Ruby. 'We don't want to put you out.'

'Oh, it's no bother,' said Sian. 'Laura will be made up to have two lots of visitors today. Please come through and I'll bring you a tray.'

The lounge was large with an ornate fireplace, comfortable-looking dining chairs and sofas that looked out onto an open courtyard.

Ruby and Adam sank down side by side on one of the sofas. Sian arrived shortly afterwards with a tea tray and scones, warm from the oven.

'This is like a luxury hotel,' enthused Ruby, spreading a thick layer of clotted cream over her scone after they'd been left alone.

'Mmm,' mumbled Adam, who was ahead of Ruby and already tucking into his.

'I think I'll go and use the restroom to freshen up,' said Ruby when they'd munched their way through a couple of scones each. 'My fingers are a bit sticky.'

She stood up and stretched. Her legs were aching slightly from her run and the long walk. She'd need another warm shower when she got back.

'Any thoughts on where the restrooms might be?' she asked Adam.

'I think I saw a sign in the corridor,' he said, pouring himself another cup of tea from the pot.

'OK, thanks.'

Ruby headed out to the wide entrance hall and looked about. She couldn't see the sign Adam was talking about and she was about to turn back when she realised someone was coming down the stairs towards her.

'Excuse me,' she called, 'do you know where I'd find the restrooms?'

The man on the stairs stopped in his

tracks. He stared at her for a long moment and then dropped the tray he was carrying. Cups and plates fell to the carpet with a thud, and a saucer rolled down to Ruby's feet. The man just stood and stared at her, open-mouthed.

'Oh my goodness, are you all right?' Ruby asked, slightly unnerved by the situation. She should call Sian for help. Was this one of the residents, having some kind of fit?

The man slowly shook his head, closed his eyes and then opened them again.

'Surely it can't be,' he whispered.

'Can't be what?' asked Ruby.

The man took a few more steps but he'd obviously forgotten about the fallen cups and stumbled down the last couple of stairs.

Ruby reached out to grab him and then gasped in surprise as she saw his face close up.

'Mother,' said the man. 'Is that you?'

16

'I feel so silly . . . ' The man laughed in embarrassment, shaking his head.

There really is no need,' said Ruby, back in the dining room and seated once more on the comfortable sofas.

'But to think you were my mother when you're so clearly young enough to be my daughter or maybe even my granddaughter — '

'It was the shock,' said Ruby, who couldn't take her eyes off her new acquaintance's face. His eyes were like Pops', a clear, brilliant blue.

Since they'd met in the hallway moments ago Sian had ushered them into the dining room while she cleared up the mess. They hadn't got round to discussing why the man had been so convinced Ruby was his mother — or why his eyes were so like Pops' — but Ruby knew.

This was Dylan Turner. Her grandfather's younger brother.

'You do look remarkably like my mother,' said Dylan, smiling at Ruby and looking even more like Pops when he did so. 'It's all that beautiful hair of yours. Hers was exactly the same. I used to bury my face in it when I was younger. Especially when I was in trouble with my father — I think I thought he couldn't see me in it.'

'Well,' said Ruby, leaning forward in her seat, aware that what she was about to say would come as a big shock to Dylan. 'I think there's a reason I look so like your mother.'

'Oh?' Dylan copied her movement.

'Are you Dylan Turner?' asked Ruby.

Dylan nodded solemnly.

'My name is Ruby Turner,' she said slowly.

She had no idea how Dylan and Alwyn had parted company. Had it been on good terms, or had Dylan rejected Alwyn after he was found guilty of manslaughter? The fact that he had probably been visiting Laura might mean he was on her side when it came to believing in Pops' guilt.

Silence greeted her statement. She let a full minute pass before opening her mouth.

'Alwyn,' Dylan stated before she could say anything.

Ruby nodded.

'I'd always hoped . . . but after so long I'd given up. Where is he? Is he with you?'

Dylan looked around the dining room which was empty save for the three of them.

Ruby hadn't given any thought to how she was going to break the news of Pops' death to someone who had loved him. It was clear from Dylan's hopeful gaze that he cared deeply for his brother. This was going to be hard.

She reached across and took Dylan's hands.

'I'm so sorry,' she said, 'but Alwyn, my beloved Pops, passed away in January.'

Watching Dylan's face crumple was one of the saddest things Ruby had ever seen. Whatever the reason for the lack of communication between the two brothers, Dylan wasn't the cause of it; he'd clearly loved his brother. She kept her hands on his and his gaze dropped to where they touched.

A few shuddering breaths told Ruby all she needed to know. After a moment or two, he turned his hands and squeezed hers.

'Tell me,' Dylan said, 'exactly who was Alwyn to you?'

'Alwyn was my grandfather. My mother, Ceri, was his only daughter. He never told us anything about his past. After his death we wanted to know more about him as a younger man, which is why I'm here.'

Dylan nodded a few times and then he took a deep breath and let it out slowly.

'I always wondered where he went after he left Wales. I'm guessing from your accent he went to America. I've tried so many times to find him and since the digital age my daughters have tried as well. But we've never had any luck, until now.'

He smiled at Ruby, a big sunshine smile that came straight from the heart. 'I feel so blessed to have met you. We can meet again, can't we?'

'Of course,' said Ruby. 'I want to know everything about you and your family. How exciting to find Mom has cousins. She's going to be so thrilled. I hope you don't mind, but I'd also like to know everything you know about Pops.'

'Of course you want to know. Let me take you out for dinner,' said Dylan. 'I'm staying at a hotel nearby. I come down once a year to see Laura and to have a look around. Originally I was looking for any trace of my brother, but when that proved fruitless it became almost a pilgrimage. Something I had to do to respect my family's memory, if that makes sense.'

'It does, and we'd love to come to dinner — but, oh, I'd forgotten we were going to see Laura!' Ruby glanced at Adam who had been silent during the exchange.

'I'll go and see Laura,' said Adam. 'I'll leave you two to catch up over dinner, and I'll come and pick you up in a few hours.'

'Are you sure?' asked Ruby, who was torn. She desperately wanted to hear what Dylan had to say, but she was reluctant to be parted from Adam after the day they'd had.

'I'm sure.' Adam smiled at her reassuringly.

They arranged to meet outside Dylan's hotel in three hours' time. Ruby followed Adam into the hallway.

'I'm sorry about this,' she said to him. 'It's not how I was hoping today would end.'

Adam leaned down and gave her a brief kiss. 'It's not ended yet,' he murmured.

She grinned and watched him bound up the stairs. She was so lucky she'd met him.

She would have liked to have spent the evening with Adam in a cosy restaurant where she could distract him from his friend's wedding some more . . . but she couldn't miss this opportunity.

★ ★ ★

As she picked up a menu in a nearby pub, she realised she was very fortunate. A few minutes earlier or later, and she would have missed Dylan altogether.

On the way to the pub Ruby had given Dylan a potted history of Alwyn's life after he'd moved to the States. Dylan had been very surprised to find out his brother had taught students English literature. He'd always imagined Alwyn would have been involved in sport somehow.

'Now it's your turn,' said Ruby, after they'd ordered their food. 'I want to know everything.'

They'd only known each other an hour but already they'd become firm friends.

'I'm a lot younger than Alwyn,' said Dylan, grinning. 'I mean, that's obvious just by looking at me.'

Ruby laughed. Dylan was slimmer and slightly shorter than Pops, but their eyes were the same and his mannerisms made him seem more like his brother than he had appeared when Ruby had first met him.

'He was ten years my senior and I idolised him. I probably got on his nerves following him about, but he never showed it. He taught me to read — and to fish.'

'Me too.' Ruby felt her eyes fill with tears.

'Aye, he was a lovely, kind boy, my brother. My mother and he were close. She was devastated when they lost contact. She believed right until the end of her life that she would see him again before she died.'

'I don't understand how they lost contact,' ventured Ruby.

'I was only nine at the time of that terrible summer and I didn't really understand what was happening and how life-changing it would all be. Things have become confused in my mind as time has passed, but I'll tell you what I remember and what I've pieced together since.'

Dylan paused as two plates were placed in front of them. Ruby had gone for a summer vegetable stew. She needed something filling after the amount of exercise she'd done today. She tucked in; it was a delicious combination of roasted chicken and new potatoes cooked in a light tomato sauce with courgettes and aubergines. After her time in the café's kitchen, she had a new appreciation for good food.

Dylan poured them both a glass of crisp, fresh wine and she took a long sip. She felt it slide down her throat, relaxing muscles as she swallowed. Bliss.

'Alwyn was devastated by the loss of his friend, Charles,' Dylan said when he'd also taken a long sip of his wine. 'The day his death happened was the only time in my life that I ever saw

Alwyn cry. It didn't take long after Charles disappeared for Laura to start telling everyone that Alwyn had killed her brother. She said they were always arguing and that Alwyn had obviously taken things too far during one of their bust-ups. No one who knew my brother believed he would kill anyone on purpose but they did know how strong he was. It wasn't hard for people to imagine he had accidentally punched Charles too hard.'

Ruby shook her head vigorously.

'Pops was the gentlest person I know despite his size. I don't believe he would have punched anyone, even by accident.'

'Aye, you're right there. He wouldn't hurt a fly. He was the one who'd carry spiders out of the house and find them somewhere nice to spin their webs. Anyway, Laura wasn't the only one who had heard them arguing a lot that summer. Despite there being no witnesses to what happened, the villagers soon took it as fact that Alwyn and

240

Charles argued and then fought physically.

'It was very unfair because no one had ever seen Alwyn, or Charles for that matter, ever get physical with anyone and certainly not with each other. I didn't see much of Charles but when I did it was clear that the two were firm friends.'

Dylan took a long sip of his wine and continued, 'Alwyn strenuously denied that he had hit Charles and that they'd not only not argued that day but that it was the first time in a long time they had been perfectly in accord. He always maintained that he hadn't seen Charles go overboard but no one believed him. He was sentenced to five years for manslaughter but he got out early because he was so well-behaved.'

'Did you ever find out what they were arguing about?' asked Ruby.

'I asked him at the time. I remember sitting with him the night before his trial began. I was crying and begging him to tell me what they'd been fighting about. He told me that they'd only ever fought about trivial things.

'He did suggest that Charles was upset about something, and that Charles kept taking it out on Alwyn by provoking him into arguments. But Alwyn said that none of the things they argued about was serious enough that would have caused them to have an actual physical fight. I can remember thinking at the time that I'd like to know what Charles was upset about, but I thought I'd have years left to find out the truth. But that was the last night I ever saw Alwyn.'

Dylan swallowed and took another sip of wine.

Ruby speared a potato and frowned.

'I have so many questions I don't know where to start.' She popped the potato in her mouth and chewed thoughtfully. 'OK, here's my first one — was Charles's body ever found?'

'Yes, the body washed up on the very beach the two girls had been sunbathing on, two months after the day he disappeared. That was when Alwyn was arrested for manslaughter, although people had decided he was guilty before that. People had started to avoid talking to us in the street and my father was let go from his job up at the manor. It was a terrible time for our family. My mother even pulled me out of school because other children started picking on me.

'I didn't mind. I was ready to fight with anyone who accused my brother of murder but I guess Mother didn't want me to get a reputation as a fighter. It wouldn't have looked good for Alwyn if members of his family were known to fly into rages.' Dylan smiled weakly.

'What proof was there that Pops had done anything wrong?' asked Ruby.

'It was all circumstantial. The major point was that Charles and Alwyn were seen arguing a lot prior to Charles' death. Of course, the fact that Alwyn was the only one with Charles at the time he died didn't do him any favours. The real nail in the coffin was the injuries on my brother's hands. Alwyn had grazes on his knuckles that he claimed were from falling while he was clambering over rocks shouting for Charles. The prosecutors claimed this was evidence that Alwyn had been in a fight.'

Ruby took another sip of wine as she thought over this new piece of information. The grazes were incriminating, but they could be explained. Was she being overly biased when she believed Pops' explanation? Very possibly.

'How is it that you never saw Alwyn again after the night before his trial?' asked Ruby.

'He went straight to prison after it ended. I didn't know until years afterwards that my mother went to visit him. I guess she felt that prison wasn't the place for young boys.' Dylan smiled sadly. 'I wished I'd known. I would have given anything to see him and maybe if I'd insisted, things might have ended differently, but it wasn't to be.

'My father was so angry. He was furious that he'd lost his job and I'm afraid he blamed Alwyn. He didn't believe he was innocent. Oh, he knew Alwyn would never plan to kill anyone but, like everyone else, he thought he had underestimated his own strength.

'Eventually Father got a job in England and we moved away from the area. I expected my brother to come and join us after he was released, but he never did. I found out years later that my father wrote to him and told him he wasn't welcome.'

'What a terrible thing to do!' exclaimed Ruby, furious on behalf of her grandfather.

Dylan nodded. 'I can't imagine cutting any of my girls out of my life. It wouldn't matter what they had done. I would always want them with me, but it was a different era then. My father felt the shame of Alwyn's jail sentence strongly. I know he regretted his harsh actions in later years. Father confessed to me that Alwyn had written to my mother for several years around Christmas and her birthday but that he'd destroyed the letters and not told her. Eventually Alwyn stopped writing. Even after my father died, I couldn't tell my mother that it was his fault we never heard from Alwyn. I don't think her heart could have taken it. I searched so hard for him in her final years. It was her greatest wish that they be reunited.'

Ruby felt her eyes fill with tears again. Poor Pops, thinking that his mother had abandoned him when in fact she'd pined for him for years and now he'd never know the truth.

'I'm going to imagine them together again now,' continued Dylan. Seeing the expression on Ruby's face he said, 'Shall we talk about happy things? Why don't you tell me about yourself and your family, and I'll tell you about mine.'

Ruby brightened and told him more details about her upbringing, and the love and laughter with which Pops had filled her childhood. In return Dylan told her about his own family. He was married with three daughters, the youngest not much older than Ruby. The eldest had two children, whom Dylan adored. His middle daughter had recently married. Dylan pulled out his wallet and showed Ruby a picture of him and his family dressed up in their finery at the wedding. Ruby smiled as she looked at Dylan, nearly bursting with pride next to his beautiful daughters and smiling wife.

As they were finishing their dessert, Dylan's phone rang. 'Ah,' he said, 'that will be my wife phoning to check up on me. I'll text her to say I'll call shortly but I'm having dinner with my niece. That will send her into a fever of curiosity.' He grinned and winked at Ruby. 'I like to keep her guessing. It keeps her keen.'

'How long have you been married?' asked Ruby.

'Forty-five years. Ah yes, I was right. She's texted me straight back with an order to phone her right now and explain myself.' Dylan chortled and slid his phone back into his jacket pocket.

'Let's walk to my hotel. Your young man will be there shortly to pick you up.'

The hotel was only a few doors away and Ruby could see that Adam's sleek car was already outside. Her heart raced with excitement at the thought of being alone with him again.

'Why do you visit Laura?' asked Ruby as they walked the short distance.

'At first I went to visit her out of curiosity. Like you, I wanted to know everything she knew about Alwyn and Charles. I quickly found out that everything she knew was coloured by her love for her brother and I didn't find out anything new.

'Then I realised how lonely she was. She has no family left and not many friends. Now I go to keep her company and to remind myself that although I lost my brother, I am still lucky enough to be surrounded by a loving family.'

Ruby nodded; she'd felt much the same about Laura when she'd called on her. She would go back before she left for the States and take some flowers, as she'd promised herself she would.

'I have one final question,' she said.

'That sounds very ominous, my dear. I hope that we have many conversations and many questions between us to come,' said Dylan warmly.

'Of course we do,' said Ruby, so pleased to have met this dear man. 'This is my final question for tonight.'

'In that case, please go ahead.'

'Do you think that Pops did it? I mean we both know he would never have killed someone deliberately but do you think he did it by accident? I wouldn't love him any less if he did.'

Dylan stopped walking and turned to face her. He took her hands in his and regarded her with the same steely gaze Pops had used if she ever needed reassurance.

'There is not,' he said firmly, 'a shadow of doubt in my mind that Alwyn is innocent. He did not kill anyone, either deliberately or acciden-tally.'

Those were the words Ruby wanted to hear but it was no good. Despite Ruby's own strong feelings, it did look as if Pops was somehow involved in young Charles Henry's death.

17

Ruby wiped over the kitchen table for what was probably the penultimate time. She could hear laughter and chatting coming from the café and knew it was time for her to join everyone. For the moment, though, she wanted to say her private goodbye to a room in which so much had happened.

In the three and a half months she'd been living in Wales she'd met some fabulous people and learned some great new skills, even though the perfect lemon drizzle cake was still beyond her grasp. She hadn't found out everything about Pops' life, but she knew enough and although she was sad that he'd had some difficult times, she couldn't regret what had happened. Had he not gone to jail, he wouldn't have moved to the States and met Grams. Ruby truly believed that Pops had enjoyed every minute with his American family and she hoped that had more than made up for the sad years he'd endured.

She dropped her cloth into the sink and made her way to the café door. She was having a goodbye party, and it was time for her to join in with her guests.

She stepped through the café door and was immediately enveloped in a large, warm, floral-scented hug.

'There you are, my lovely girl. I was about to send Adam to look for you. We were beginning to think you'd done a bunk.'

Ruby grinned at her newly discovered Aunt Helen, who was incredibly affectionate and always went out of her way to make Ruby feel welcomed and loved by her new family.

'I wouldn't miss my own party,' she said, disentangling herself from Dylan's wife and leaning forward to kiss Dylan on the cheek.

Dylan's family had been a delightful surprise she hadn't been expecting when she'd come to Wales. She'd met

Helen first and been struck by how similar she was to Grams — not just physically but in personality too. It seemed the Turner brothers had similar taste when it came to women.

When Ruby had introduced Helen and Grams via Skype, they had taken to each other in a big way. Now they were calling and texting each other every few days. They'd already arranged for Grams to come and stay with them in Wales after Christmas. Plans were also being made for Dylan and Helen to come to the States and to stay with Ruby's family for a month, probably during the following summer.

Ruby had met all her second cousins and was completely besotted with Dylan's two young grandchildren. It was going to be a huge wrench to say goodbye to them all at the end of the party. She didn't know when she'd see the cousins again.

She'd also become fond of some of her regular customers and she was touched that so many of them had come to her party to wish her well. The farewells to them all would be tough, but none of that sadness would be comparable to the goodbye she was going to have to say to the man standing on the other side of the café, deep in conversation with Estelle. Adam.

She felt her throat thicken at the thought, but she would not cry. She was not going to spoil their last night together with tears.

Their summer together had been beautiful. They'd both been working hard but they'd made as much time as possible to spend together. They'd not talked about the future until a few days ago. They had taken a picnic supper to the beach and lain on the sand basking in the fading sun.

'I don't want this to be it,' Ruby had whispered over the swish of the incoming tide.

'Me neither,' he'd said and then he'd rolled to face her. 'I'm sure we can make this work.'

He'd threaded his fingers into her

hair and gently tugged her face to his. They'd kissed deeply and Ruby had felt so hopeful but later, when they'd sat down to work out their schedules, things hadn't gone well. Adam had submitted his latest novel and was already at work on the next. He'd planned to be halfway through the new manuscript when he was expected to go on a world tour to promote the one he'd been writing when he and Ruby first met. Ruby was committed to teaching during the school term, and she had her own academic book deadline to complete. The first time they could get together for any length of time was the following summer.

'It's too long apart. It will never work,' Ruby had said, hoping Adam would argue with her but he hadn't. Instead he'd pulled her close and murmured his agreement.

Later, as they sat with fingers entwined, Ruby said, 'If we're going to split at the end of the summer then it has to be a clean break. Neither of us wants messy text messages and teary phone calls. I won't contact you.'

Adam had smiled sadly down at her. 'If that's what you want then I'll agree.'

It wasn't what she wanted. She wanted him to say he would come and live with her in the States but she knew his family and friends were all here in Britain and she'd never ask him to make such a sacrifice. Besides, he'd not asked her to stay in Wales, so maybe the strong feelings were all on her side.

She made her way to him now. If she wasn't going to see him after tomorrow, then she wanted to spend as much time with him as she could.

He held out his arm to her as she approached and she let herself be tugged to his side. She breathed in his familiar citrus smell and leaned her head against his chest.

Estelle didn't comment on their familiarity but her eyes twinkled knowingly.

'Estelle was just updating me on the Charles Henry poems,' Adam said.

'Yes, that's right,' said the house manager with enthusiasm. 'The Maurice Henry

Foundation is absolutely over the moon with your discovery. The poems are sublime and Laura has agreed that we can get them published. We found a publisher for them straight away and the buzz around them is quite extraordinary. It's given Laura a new lease of life and there's talk of her being at the launch party, which we hope to have here at the manor. She's not left that care home for at least ten years, so this is quite something. Well done you for finding them.'

Ruby smiled, happy at the thought of giving Laura some much-needed joy. Ruby had been to see the old lady several times. She'd confessed to being Alwyn's granddaughter but they'd quickly glossed over the revelation; she suspected Laura didn't want to lose one of her few visitors. Instead they focused on their shared love of Melveryn Manor and the newly discovered poetry.

Ruby had taken flowers and cake on her visits and Laura had seemed to genuinely enjoy her company. Alwyn was never discussed between them again.

The party seemed to go on for hours
and yet it was over in a flash. In no time
at all Ruby was hugging her new family
who were half-crying and half-laughing
over their goodbyes. Dylan and Helen
were the last of her guests to leave.

'I'm so glad to have met you,' said
Dylan, his hands resting on her
shoulders. 'You and your family have
already brought so much joy to our
lives and I feel contented knowing that
Alwyn had a good life. You must come
and visit us soon.'

Ruby nodded and agreed that she
would visit as soon as possible, even
though she knew it would be at least a
year before she could even think about
planning a trip. She would come,
though, that much was certain. Now
that she'd found her extended family
she wouldn't let them go.

Eventually Dylan and Helen stepped
outside. Ruby stood in the doorway
waving goodbye until they disappeared

out of sight. Then there was only silence left and the scuff of Adam's shoes against the floor as he moved towards her. Choking back tears, she couldn't turn to face him.

He stopped when he reached her back and his hands slid along her arms.

'How are you doing?' he asked.

'Mm,' she managed. Her throat felt thick with unshed tears.

'That bad, huh?'

'Right now I can't remember why I want to return home,' she said quietly.

Adam shuddered behind her and she wasn't sure if the movement came from a laugh or a sob; possibly it was both. He slowly turned her round until her face was pressed against his chest. She wrapped her arms around his neck and he slid his around her waist.

The stood, pressed together, breathing in one another's scent for a long time.

She wanted to tell him how, over the last two months, his existence had become integral to her being and how she couldn't imagine living without him, but for once she couldn't find her voice.

He'd not given any indication that he felt as deeply as her, so she kept all her feelings inside. Instead she threaded her fingers into the hair at the back of his neck and pulled his mouth down to hers. If she couldn't tell him how much she loved him then she would show him.

18

The manor house was bleak without Ruby. The six weeks since she'd left had been long and painful. Adam still had another five months on his lease, but he simply didn't think he'd be able to stick it out.

He was off on a promotional tour of his latest novel for the next six weeks, and then it would be Christmas. The thought of coming back to the silent house after holidaying with his parents during the festive period filled him with depression. He made a note in his diary to talk to Estelle; maybe he could break his lease early.

In the first few days after Ruby had returned to the States he'd kidded himself that he'd be fine without her. He'd been with Clara for eight years when they split up and he'd survived, hurt more by the aftermath of their break-up than by the loss of his fiancée. He'd only been with Ruby around eight weeks, which was nothing. They had virtually no shared history and they'd not met one another's friends or family — apart from her newfound relatives. But the difference he'd felt after the two break-ups was extreme.

It felt as if a black hole had opened up in the place Ruby had occupied and nothing he did seemed to fill it.

When Ruby had suggested a clean break he'd agreed with her. It was the sensible solution. The break-up would be so much worse if he rang to beg her to come back to him, only to find she'd already moved on. He just hadn't expected it to be so difficult not to contact her.

He'd never had the urge to call Clara after the end of their relationship, but he thought about speaking to Ruby every few minutes. He'd be typing and suddenly think of something she'd find funny, and have to fight the instinct to reach for his phone and tap out a message to her.

Their brief relationship was over, and the sooner his mind accepted it, the better it would be for his mental health.

He'd been sitting at his computer for more than two hours and he'd only managed a few lines. He read them over and then deleted them. It was all total rubbish. He pushed back from his desk, rubbing his shoulder, and stood up abruptly. He needed a break from trying to force the story out.

He should pack. He was off around Britain for the next few days. He was booked to speak at a couple of conventions and then he was doing an interview with a major radio station.

He felt sick whenever he thought about the radio. It was one thing to give a talk to a roomful of people; quite another to speak to millions of people at one time. It was all to promote his new book in time for the Christmas market. As soon as he finished in Britain, he was off to Australia for ten days. Hopefully the sun would help his bleak mood.

After that, he was going to the States

for a three-week tour. The nearest he would get to Ruby was a two-hour drive from her home. One evening, when he'd been feeling particularly low, he'd mapped the route, even though he knew he wouldn't be taking it.

He shook his head. He must stop thinking about Ruby.

His phone rang and he grabbed it with unseemly speed. It was Nick.

'Hey,' he said, hoping his voice didn't betray his disappointment.

'Hi mate,' said Nick. 'I'm ringing to check you're still OK for Saturday.'

As part of Adam's tour he was going to be very close to Nick and Clara's new home in Bristol. He'd promised to call in and see them, even though it was the last thing he wanted to do. If he wanted to keep his relationship with Nick going he knew he needed to make an effort — and there was always going to be a first time he would have to see Clara again.

Hopefully it would be like ripping off a plaster; painful but ultimately a step forward. There was no getting away from the fact that it was going to be awkward. He tried not to think how much easier the visit would be if Ruby was going with him for support. Frustrated by how soon Ruby had appeared in his thoughts again, he banged his head against a nearby wall.

'Are you all right?' asked a concerned Nick.

'Yeah. Sorry about the noise, I tripped. Yes, I'm fine for Saturday, and looking forward to seeing you both.'

Nick snorted. 'I'm sure you're not — but hopefully it will be less awkward than we're all expecting it to be.'

Adam laughed and they chatted for a few more minutes before clicking off. He felt a bit better after speaking to his friend. Hopefully Saturday wouldn't be too excruciating and after that first step was made, then they could all move forward.

Adam headed through to his bedroom and pulled two suitcases out from under his bed. He wouldn't have time to come back to Wales after his tour of Britain and before his trip to Australia, and so he needed to pack for both trips now.

Luckily he wouldn't have to take the same clothes to both places and he'd leave the spare suitcase with his parents, who lived on the outskirts of London, not far from Heathrow. He'd be back in London before his trip to the States and he'd probably need a mixture of both clothes for his trip there.

He wondered wryly if he was too old to ask his parents to do his washing while he was away. He decided he probably was, but then again it wouldn't hurt to ask.

He filled his British suitcase with warm clothes and a waterproof jacket in case there was time for some walking. Zipping that up, he moved on to packing for Australia. It was going to be summer out there so he put shorts and T-shirts in.

He checked the bureau in the corner of the room, but he couldn't find the flight tickets. He knew he'd brought them into his bedroom a few days ago, ready to go into his bags. He pulled out the drawers but he hadn't put them away in there. Perhaps they'd fallen behind the bureau. He rested his head against the wall and tried to peer down the back, but it was too dark.

He pushed the piece of furniture forward and to his relief, he found the tickets resting on top of a curl of peeling wallpaper. He pulled them out and slid them into the front pocket of his suitcase. He was done with packing for today. He'd head back to his office to see whether the break from writing had helped with his writer's block, but first he needed to put the bureau back into position.

A thick layer of dust had built up on the peeling wallpaper, which was normally hidden from sight. Should he pull off the flap of paper, or dust it? He decided it wasn't his place to remove wallpaper in this historic house, so he fetched a duster and gave it a quick swipe.

Then he saw what looked like a corner of an envelope underneath the wallpaper. He touched it. It moved slightly; it wasn't attached to the wall.

He managed to get his thumb and forefinger around the edges and gave a gentle tug. As he pulled, the envelope came away easily. The paper was yellowing and the flap had come unstuck.

Slowly he turned the envelope round, and found with a jolt that he recognised the writing on the front. He'd read many poems written in the same neat hand. This was a letter from Charles Henry . . . but it was the addressee that had Adam's heart racing. Across the front of the envelope, the name *Alwyn Turner* was written in bold strokes.

For a moment Adam debated whether or not to read what was inside. It wasn't his place to read this correspondence. But what if he sent it to Ruby, and it turned out to be simply a letter sent from Charles to Alwyn while he was at school?

In the end, curiosity won and Adam

pulled out the letter. What he read had him raising his eyebrows. This was something Ruby and her family should definitely see.

He returned the letter to the envelope and pondered his next move. He could post the letter — he had Ruby's American address — but what if the letter got lost en route? Its contents were too important. He'd take the letter to her.

It was only a four-hour round trip to her house from where he'd be giving a promotional talk. That was nothing in America. It wouldn't give Adam long with Ruby — but he had plenty of time to plan what he was going to say to her.

Life suddenly seemed so much better than it had at any point in the last six weeks. At last he had a reason to see Ruby . . . and he wouldn't waste the opportunity.

19

Ruby had been so worried that the bookshop would be empty, but she needn't have wasted her energy. Instead of the empty space she'd been concerned about, the place was heaving. She and Grams were lucky to get inside the store.

'There's a space near the front,' hissed Grams, as Ruby tugged her towards the back.

'I told you before we left that I was going to stay near the back,' Ruby responded.

'I don't understand why it's so important,' said Grams, as Ruby found them both chairs and indicated that Grams should take one.

Ruby sank into her seat, pleased to see that the man in front of her was very tall. The chances of her being spotted in this crowd were minimal.

Grams settled into her seat, looking around.

'Well, this is exciting,' she said.

Ruby glanced up to the raised platform at the front of the shop. It was empty apart from two chairs and a small round table. She checked her watch. The talk was due to start in ten minutes.

Next to her, Grams pulled a book out of her handbag and rested it on her knees.

'What did you bring that for?' asked Ruby, horrified, when she saw it.

'I thought there might be time to get it signed,' said Grams, beaming at her.

'Grams, have you listened to a word I've said?' asked Ruby, exasperated.

'I have, darling,' said Grams, patting her knee. 'I've brought the book in case you feel differently after seeing him — because although you've gone through your reasoning many times, I still don't understand why you can't speak to him. If, after you've seen him give his talk, you still don't want to, then of course we'll get back in your car and go home. You won't get any arguments from me.'

'Thanks, Grams,' said Ruby, relieved.

'It's a shame, though — I've always wanted to meet him.'

Grams grinned at Ruby's frustrated face.

'I'm teasing you, darling. I don't understand why we can't say 'hello' to him. What's the use of coming to see a famous author if I can't get a book signed by him? But if that's what you want then I'm not going to go on.'

Ruby shook her head. She knew that Grams wasn't going to force her to stand in line for the book signing, but she didn't believe for a minute that Grams wouldn't go on about it.

Fortunately the gentleman seated next to Grams wanted to discuss the book she was holding, so Ruby could sit in silence and watch the stage. She couldn't imagine coming out to face all these people. It was all right to give a lecture to students, Ruby did that regularly, but she wasn't promoting her own work. If she was waiting in the wings to talk to this crowd, she'd be a bag of nerves.

A young woman bounced onto the stage.

'Good afternoon, everyone and thank you to all of you for coming along to our store today. It gives me great pleasure to welcome our guest, the best-selling crime writer, Adam Jacobs.'

The crowd burst into applause as a smiling Adam made his way onto the stage. A local radio star followed him and they both took their seats while the clapping continued.

Despite her desire not to be spotted Ruby leaned forward to get a better look at him. He'd had his hair cut. It was shorter at the sides and looked neater than it had over the summer. He was wearing dark jeans and a navy jumper, sleeves pushed up to his elbows.

His eyes scanned the audience. For a second it felt as if they stopped on her but his gaze moved on and she sank back. Why was she even here? They'd agreed to have no contact after the end of the summer and she'd stuck to that, even though it had been very hard. There had been many times during the fall semester when she'd considered resigning from her job and jumping on a plane back to Wales to be with him.

The only thing that had stopped her was that he'd not asked her to stay with him. If she'd had so much of a text hinting that he'd like her to return, nothing would have stopped her. Not even the fact that it would ruin her hard-earned career.

When Grams had found out Adam was coming to New York, a mere two-hour car journey from their home, as part of his world tour she'd persuaded Ruby to come to his talk. At first Ruby had been reluctant but Grams had been a huge fan of Adam's books for many years and said she would go without her. In the end Ruby's desire to see him had taken over her common sense and so here she was.

The talk began and Ruby listened as Adam talked about his work. His English accent was in stark contrast to the American voices around him. He was speaking about his fictional detective, Grimes, whom she knew next to nothing about, having only read one of his novels. She was content to listen to his warm voice and she felt like a woman in a desert who had been given a long, cool drink of fresh water.

All too soon the talk was over and a line was forming of people who wanted their books signed by him. It seemed all the audience was rushing to get a place near the front.

'Are you sure we can't get his signature?' asked Grams, as Ruby began to push in the opposite direction to the tide of people.

'Please, Grams! You promised,' begged Ruby.

Whatever Grams could see on her granddaughter's face finally convinced her not to push her any more and they slipped out of the store together.

Ruby didn't realise she was shaking until she tried to put the key in the ignition and found she couldn't get it into the slot.

'Are you all right, darling?' asked Grams.

'Sure,' she answered automatically. She stopped and took a long, steadying breath.

When she felt calmer, she tried again. This time the key slid into place and she was able to start the car and pull out of her space.

She drove for a while in silence, which was uncharacteristic for both her and Grams. They were both big talkers.

'Thank you for driving me today,' said Grams eventually. 'I've had a lovely day out.'

They'd been shopping before going to Adam's talk. Grams had wanted to choose Christmas presents for all her new relatives and they'd spent a joyful morning buying gifts. It was good to see Grams looking so happy. She'd been devastated by Pops' death but finding his brother and his family had given her a new lease of life and she'd started to return to her normal self.

'I've had a lovely day too, Grams,' she said.

They drove for another half an hour in silence.

'I miss your Pops,' said Grams, suddenly breaking the silence.

'Me too,' said Ruby.

'I know, darling, but it's different for you.'

Ruby frowned; Grams didn't normally talk like this. 'What do you mean?' she asked.

'Pops was my soulmate. I was with him for forty years and our lives became so entwined that I don't know where his memories began and mine ended. Now that he's gone, it's like I've lost part of myself.'

Ruby didn't know what to say. Grams was normally such a practical person, not someone given over to sentimentality.

'What I'm trying to say,' said Grams, her tone brisker, 'is that love between a couple is special. It doesn't come often in our lives and it's something that should be cherished. If you find love, you mustn't throw it away through misguided practicalities.'

Ruby nodded slowly. Was Grams talking about Adam and herself? Was what they'd had true love or just a summer fling? She still wasn't sure.

'That's all I'm going to say on the subject,' said Grams, folding her arms on her lap.

'Is that so?' asked Ruby, a smile in her voice despite the subject matter.

'Well, maybe not,' said Grams laughing. 'But it's all I'm going to say on the matter this evening. Did you enjoy Adam's talk? I thought it was fascinating. I can't wait to read this new one. The early reviews are saying it's his best novel yet.'

'I did enjoy the talk but I didn't really understand most of what was said. I've only read one of his books for a module

I did years ago and I only skim-read it then.'

'Ruby Turner, I'm shocked at you. How can you only ever have read one?'

'Too scary,' she replied succinctly.

'Dear me, you need educating in the world of scary fiction. Have you ever read any Stephen King?' asked Grams.

'Are you kidding me? He's the scariest of all.'

Grams made Ruby laugh for the rest of the journey home. Grams was shocked that Ruby could get away with being a professor of literature without having read an entire genre of books and vowed to get her reading her favourite canon.

Ruby was grateful for the change in subject. It took her mind off Adam, how gorgeous he'd looked up on stage and how proud she was of him attracting so many supporters.

By the time they got home Ruby was ready for a bath. She still lived at her childhood address but her parents had converted the space above the garage, where she had a tiny flat with everything she needed. She dropped Grams off at the main house and agreed with her parents that she'd come back over for a late dinner after she'd had time to soak in the bubbles for a bit.

When she slid into the warm, comforting water she allowed herself a little cry. Seeing Adam had reminded her how much she missed him, but there was no going back. She'd made the decision to stop their relationship and he may have already moved on. Surely he would have contacted her if he thought they'd made a mistake but she hadn't heard a single thing from him since she'd left.

When the water turned cold she realised how long she'd been there. She jumped out and quickly dried herself. She checked in the mirror, pleased to see her eyes weren't bloodshot. She'd never get away with not telling her family what the problem was if there was evidence of tears.

She pulled on some leggings and a large comfy jumper and, not bothering with make-up, made her way over to her parents' house. She slid in through the back door and then stopped short.

There, standing tall in her parents' kitchen, was Adam.

20

'Look who's here,' said Grams, totally unnecessarily in Ruby's opinion.

'Hi,' said Ruby, lifting her hand and giving Adam a small wave.

'Hey,' said Adam, returning her wave, his lips twitching as he did so. Ruby felt laughter bubbling up inside her too.

'You must be tired after your journey,' said Grams, fluttering around Adam like a butterfly. 'Please take a seat. We were about to have dinner and you must join us.'

'Grams . . . ' said Ruby, about to interject on Adam's behalf.

'That would be lovely, thank you,' said Adam, taking the chair offered to him.

Ruby was nudged into the chair next to him by her mother. As plates and dishes were handed round, Ruby's arm brushed against Adam's and she fought the urge to lean into him.

Grams peppered Adam with questions about his writing throughout the meal and he responded good-naturedly. Despite her nerves, which normally left her rambling nonsense, Ruby found it difficult to start talking on any subject. She stayed quiet and looked at Adam whenever an opportunity in the conversation allowed her.

'Would you be so good as to sign my copy of your book?' Grams asked Adam, as the meal was drawing to a close.

'Of course,' said Adam.

'Grams is a super-fan,' murmured Ruby as Grams stood up to fetch her book.

'I am,' said Grams unashamedly.

'It's always lovely to meet a fan,' said Adam, taking the book from Grams and writing a long message in it. 'Some people aren't keen. They find my writing too scary.' He winked at Ruby.

'Those people are wimps,' said Grams traitorously.

Adam laughed and handed the book back.

'Actually,' he said, 'I've come here because I've got something to show you.'

'Me?' asked Grams, confused.

'Um, well, I guess all of you. I found something after Ruby left that will be of interest to you all.'

'What?' asked Ruby, more sharply than she intended.

'I found a letter addressed to Alwyn. Pops.'

The kitchen descended into silence.

'Who was the letter from?' asked Ruby quietly.

'It was from Charles Henry,' said Adam. 'I found it behind a desk in the room I was using as my bedroom in Melveryn Manor.'

'Why did I never think to search in your section of the house?' asked Ruby, bewildered by her oversight.

'I didn't think about it either,' said Adam. 'But I doubt we would have found it even if we'd tried. It was hidden behind some wallpaper and I only found it by accident. I have no idea how it can have got there. I didn't trust the postal company to deliver it intact so I brought it with me. Its contents are too important to you all, I think.'

Adam rummaged in the bag he had at his feet and straightened, holding a yellowing envelope. He held it out to no one in particular and for a moment it hung in the air. Eventually Grams took it and Ruby and her parents crowded round her so they could get a good look at its contents.

Grams' hands were shaking as she pulled the letter out of the envelope. Over Grams' shoulder Ruby read,

My dear Alwyn,

Firstly, I must apologise for being such a bore this summer. I don't know how you've put up with me and my bad temper. You've been a great friend to me, one that I don't deserve.

I know that you don't agree with me that what I've done is that bad, but it is preying on my conscience. I don't think I can live with the shame even though you are the only person who knows the whole truth.

The future looks like a long, unending, dark tunnel from which I can see no escape. I don't want to live like this any more. I'm hoping that in death I will find some peace. So, my friend, I owe you another apology because we had so many plans for our future and now you'll be doing them without me. I think, after what I've done, that is for the best.

I'm leaving this letter for you but I hope that you will tell my sister that death is what I wanted. Tell her that I am sorry to cause her any pain.

Please, live well, my dear Alwyn.
Yours, Charles

'Oh my,' said Grams softly. 'The young man killed himself.'

'Poor boy,' said Ruby's mom, leaning down to give Grams a hug.

'At least now we know what happened to Charles,' said Grams, patting Mom's arms. 'Even though we'll never know what he did that caused him so much anguish. It's a shame Alwyn never read this letter while he was alive — but let's hope they're together again and that Charles is happy at last.'

Ruby squeezed Gram's shoulder and swallowed. How kind it was of Adam to have travelled so far to bring them this letter. Was it the only reason he had come?

'Thank you for the wonderful meal,' said Adam. 'I had best head back if I'm to make it in time to catch my next flight.'

Ruby was shocked. She knew he had a tight schedule but she had been expecting they'd have time to talk alone before he left. If she'd known they only had a couple of hours before he had to go again she would have insisted they ate alone in her flat. She had so much to say to him.

'It was lovely to meet you,' said Grams, standing up to shake Adam's hand. 'Thank you so much for bringing that letter. It means the world to us to know, for sure, that Alwyn had nothing to do with Charles' death.'

'It was my pleasure,' said Adam. 'And thanks to you all for the lovely meal and company.'

'I'll show you to the door,' said Ruby, not wanting to say her goodbye in front of her family.

'Is your tour going well?' she asked as they walked towards her parents' front porch.

There was so much she wanted to say but she could only manage something banal.

'Good, thanks. The crowds have generally been as strong as they were this afternoon. My publishers are very pleased.'

That statement sounded as if he knew she'd seen how many people had been at his book signing today. Surely he hadn't seen her? He certainly hadn't given any indication that he'd noticed her sitting in the audience.

'I'm glad,' she said vaguely.

They'd already reached the entrance and Adam had his car keys in his hand. Her time with him was slipping away and she still couldn't find the right words to say to him.

He reached into his shoulder bag and pulled out a hard back copy of his book.

'This is for you,' he said, holding it out to her. 'I noticed you didn't buy one this afternoon.'

Heat rushed to Ruby's face. So he had seen her. What must he think of her, not making time to speak to him?

'I'm sorry I didn't come and say hello,' she murmured. 'Grams wanted to come and see you . . . not that I didn't, but . . . we said we wouldn't so I didn't, you know . . . ' Ruby stumbled over her explanation.

'It's OK, I understand,' said Adam quietly.

This encounter was not going the

way Ruby had hoped when they'd left her family in the kitchen. Adam's expression was closed and she couldn't tell what he was thinking. He was still holding the book out to her and so she took it from him.

'Thank you. I'll look forward to reading it,' she said politely.

Adam's lips twitched. 'I'm sure you won't.'

Ruby's fingers curled around the edge of the book. Adam was leaning forward to open the door but he couldn't go without her telling him how she felt.

'Adam — ' she gasped as he stepped over the threshold. She felt stricken and all the words she wanted to say stayed blocked in her throat.

Adam stood watching her; the darkness of the night surrounding him.

When she didn't say anything else he leaned down and brushed her cheek with his lips.

'Take care of yourself, Ruby,' he murmured and then he was gone.

21

Ruby lay on her bed, but she couldn't sleep. In the ten days since she'd last seen Adam she'd gone off her food and found sleep virtually impossible.

While the rest of her family had celebrated Pops' innocence she'd retreated into herself and spent most of her time at work or in her flat. The cooler weather of the fall meant she could justify spending more time indoors wearing snug, comforting pajamas and drinking lots of hot chocolate.

In the euphoria following the reading of Charles' letter it had taken her family a little while to realise she was suffering. Once they cottoned on that all was not right in Ruby's world, they tried to get her to talk about what was wrong.

Unusually for her, she hadn't wanted to talk about Adam to anyone. She kept going through the evening he'd visited in her mind. She replayed every detail of his actions, trying to work out whether his motivation for coming to visit her family was purely because of the letter or whether he'd done it to see her.

If he'd come to see her, then why hadn't he said anything? If it was purely because of the letter, then why hadn't he just sent it by courier? She couldn't settle on an answer and she was driving herself crazy.

One thing she was absolutely sure about was her own feelings. She loved Adam and she'd been a fool to let him go.

There was a knock on the flat door. Ever since her family had realised she was feeling low, they'd been taking it in turns to check up on her. It was Grams' turn this evening but she was a little later than usual.

Even though it was only nine, Ruby was already in bed. She was bone tired even though sleep was elusive. She didn't get up; Grams had a key and would let herself in.

'Hello, darling,' came Grams' cheerful voice from the entrance way.

'Hey,' called Ruby, 'I'm in my room.'

Ruby heard footsteps as Grams made her way through the flat.

'Oh, darling.' Grams came in and perching on Ruby's bed. 'I don't like to see you like this.'

'I'm just tired,' said Ruby unconvincingly.

Grams was holding a book on her lap. Ruby only needed a quick glance to know that it was Adam's. Her own copy was on her bedside table. She hadn't read it, but she couldn't bring herself to put it away on her bookshelf either. Everything about the novel threw her into emotional turmoil. She either remembered Adam writing it and the days they'd spent together, or their last disastrous conversation on her parents' porch.

She should have told him she loved him right there and then. If he didn't feel the same then the only thing she would have lost was her pride. Instead she'd been a coward, and she was furious with herself.

'What's wrong, my lovely girl?' asked Grams, stroking Ruby's hair away from her face.

Ruby thought about denying that there was a problem but Grams was one of her best friends and talking had always made her feel better in the past.

'I can't decide whether I should contact Adam to tell him I love him or not,' she said.

'You should definitely tell him,' said Grams.

Ruby pulled herself into a sitting position and leaned back against her headboard. 'Why are you so positive that's the right thing to do? What if he doesn't love me back? Won't that make me feel worse?'

'He loves you back,' said Gram firmly.

'Did he tell you that?' asked Ruby, confused. How could Grams be so sure?

'He didn't need to. It's all in here.' Grams held up her copy of Adam's latest book.

'What do you mean?' asked Ruby, taking the book from Grams and leafing through the pages. She was half expecting the words *I love Ruby* to leap out at her from the pages.

'You're Detective Grimes' new girlfriend,' said Grams.

Ruby frowned. What was Grams talking about?

'Who's Detective Grimes?'

'Detective Grimes is the main character in Adam's latest series. For the last six books he's been single with not a hint of any romance but in this one he meets a girl. You're that girl.'

'In what way?' asked Ruby, still not seeing how she could be a fictional character in a murder mystery.

'In a good way. Amber, that's the girlfriend's name, is warm, vivacious, bright and sparkly, which is just like you.'

Ruby smiled. 'Thanks, Grams, but that could describe a whole host of women I know. The character doesn't have to be based on me.'

Grams snorted. 'It's you all right and the person who wrote those words did so full of love. Adam loves you.'

'He's a talented writer. He doesn't have to be in love with a person to write about love. Otherwise it would mean he is also capable of the most gruesome murders — and I know that he isn't.' Ruby shuddered.

'Surely the name Amber is enough to convince you. He couldn't call her Ruby so he called her by another semi-precious stone instead. It's so obvious.'

Ruby opened her mouth to protest but Grams held up her hand to stop her.

'Read it and then you'll see exactly what I mean. I'll even do you a deal. I'll stay in the lounge and watch *Downton Abbey* on catch-up while you read it and if you get scared, you can come and sit with me.'

Ruby was about to argue that she was too old to need comforting after a scary story, but then she remembered how she'd felt after only two pages of one of Adam's books. She would feel better if Grams stayed, so in the end she didn't protest.

She heard Grams settle on the sofa and the quiet murmur of voices started up as she found the programme she was looking for.

Ruby picked up her copy of the book. It was thick and heavy and encased in a dark dust jacket with Adam's name embossed in large letters across the front cover. She turned to the inside flap and looked at his author picture. He was so beautiful. She ran her fingers across his familiar face. It didn't matter whether or not he'd written her into his book, she needed to contact him somehow and tell him that she loved him. Even if he didn't love her back, he deserved to know how she felt. With her decision made, she felt calmer than she had in days.

She turned to the front flap and read the blurb. It sounded as scary as the rest of his novels, but she'd told Gran she'd give it a go and so she started to turn the pages.

When she got to the title page she stopped. Adam had handwritten her a message that she'd not seen before. She read it once, and then again.

'Grams,' she called, stumbling out of bed in an effort to share her news.

'You can't be scared already!' said Grams, coming quickly to her room. 'You've only just started reading. Oh my, what are you doing?'

Ruby was racing around the room trying to find some clean clothes and a large bag.

'You were right,' said Ruby, as she pulled a backpack out from her closet. 'He does love me!'

'OK, but why are you now running around in a crazed manner?' asked Grams bewilderedly.

'I'm going to him,' Ruby said as she threw a change of clothes into her bag.

'You're going to fly to England tonight?' Grams queried.

'I don't need to; he's still in the States.' She passed Grams a piece of paper. 'This is his touring schedule. I picked it up when we went to New York to see him and I've been following his progress around the States. His last stop is Seattle tomorrow. He'll be at Barnes and Noble at twelve. I'll meet him there.'

Grams glanced at her watch.

'I don't think you'll get a flight at this time of night. Let's look up the flight times for first thing tomorrow and see if we can find anything suitable. With the time difference, you should be able to leave here early and get there in plenty of time.'

Grams logged into Ruby's computer while Ruby continued with her frenzied packing.

'There's a flight from JFK tomorrow at six-thirty. That will get you there for about nine-thirty in the morning, west coast time. It's a quick bus ride to downtown Seattle from the airport, so that should give you plenty of time to find the bookshop and wait for him to arrive.'

'How much is the ticket?' asked Ruby, very aware how limited her funds were after her summer in Wales.

'It would be cheaper for you to make a phone call and tell him how you feel,' said Grams, turning the computer screen so Ruby could see the price.

'True,' said Ruby, grimacing as she took the laptop from Grams and started to type in her credit card details to book the flight. 'I have to see him in person, though.'

Ruby stopped typing and handed Grams her copy of the book open at the title page so Grams could read what Adam had written.

'Oh,' said Grams as she read, 'that's lovely. Yes, you do have to go — and if you need help with money, all you need to do is ask.'

'Thank you, Grams,' said Ruby, leaning over and hugging her grand-mother. 'You're the best — and thank you for making me read Adam's book.

If you hadn't, I may never have opened it and seen the message.'

'Have you read any of the actual book yet?'

'No — but I'll have plenty of time to read it on the plane tomorrow.'

22

Ruby squirmed in frustration as the doors to the bus stayed open.

Why weren't they moving? There was no one waiting to come aboard or running to catch it, and yet they'd been unmoving for what seemed like ten hours. Ruby checked her watch. Thanks to delays at JFK airport it was now half past eleven. It should take forty minutes from the airport to the bookshop, which meant she'd be ten minutes late if the bus left right now. Ten minutes late was fine. She could hang about at the back and be the last person in the line for the book signing. She didn't want an audience for what she wanted to say to Adam.

Finally, after what seemed like an eternity, the hiss of the doors sounded and they slid shut.

Ruby's legs bounced up and down as

they slowly made their way onto the highway. She didn't dare look at her watch as the miles crept slowly by, hindered by heavy traffic and a bus driver who didn't seem to have any sense of urgency.

She reached into her backpack and pulled out Adam's book. She'd read it from start to finish on the six-hour flight from New York and she'd been staggered by his writing talent. Sure, it had been very creepy in places but she'd been gripped. She didn't know whether Amber was based on her or not. Grams seemed to think so but Ruby didn't recognise herself in the feisty and sure-footed heroine. She couldn't imagine Amber making a hash out of telling the man she loved that he was the only one for her. Amber wouldn't be sitting on a bus uncomfortable with nerves. She would already be with her man. Ruby shook her head. It didn't matter whether Amber was based on her or not; what mattered was Adam's written message meant only for her.

Ruby turned to the front of the book and read the words again, even though she already had them memorised.

Ruby,
My life was empty of colour, then you burst onto the scene like the brightest of fireworks. You make everything and everyone around you sparkle with joy. I love you, Ruby. Shine brightly. Yours, Adam.

There was nothing in the message to suggest that he thought she might feel the same way. He had written the note, not with the expectation that she would love him too, but with the desire to let her know how he felt. It made her love him even more. He'd been brave, and now he must think that she didn't care for him. A phone call definitely wasn't enough. She needed to look into his eyes when she told him that she loved him.

The bus wheezed into Westlake Station. Ruby was already on her feet when it came to a shuddering stop at the terminal. She shot off the bus and ran to the exit. A big clock situated high on the wall told her that Adam had been giving his talk for a little over half an hour. How long had he been talking about his book when she'd seen him? Maybe forty minutes, with ten minutes for questioning at the end but then there was the book signing afterwards? She could still make it.

She stood at the exit for the station; which way should she go? She ran over to a young woman walking with a toddler.

'Excuse me,' she said. 'Please can you tell me which way it is to Barnes and Noble?'

'Sure, it's in the Pacific Place mall, which is one block that way,' said the woman, pointing in the opposite direction to which they were facing.

'Thank you,' called Ruby as she sprinted away.

It took her under a minute to reach the mall and to find the bookshop on the corner with its entrance facing out onto the street. She took a moment to catch her breath before stepping inside the air-conditioned store.

The shop was empty.

Where were the crowds of people? Stunned, she walked around the store. Could it be that somewhere in here was a hidden room? She found a worker stacking chairs.

'Adam Jacobs,' were the only words Ruby could manage.

'Aw, honey, you've missed him.'

'But he was supposed to be talking at twelve. It's only a few minutes after half past,' Ruby protested.

'Sorry, honey, we moved the talk to earlier this morning. The notification was on our website but I'm so sorry you missed him. We've got a few signed copies left if you'd like to buy one.'

Ruby shook her head. 'I've got one, thanks.'

She turned to walk away and then turned back as she thought of some-thing.

'Why did you move the talk forward?' she asked.

'He needed to catch a flight so he asked us a while ago to change the time. I'm so sorry, you look devastated. Are you a big fan?'

'Yes.' Ruby nodded. 'I'm a huge fan.'

'I think it's hard to be a fan when you haven't read any of the books,' said a deep voice from behind her.

Ruby swung round. Adam was standing behind her, a wheeled suitcase at his side. His lips were twitching as if he was fighting a smile but his eyes remained serious.

'Is everything OK, Mr Jacobs?' asked the store assistant.

'I left my rucksack here,' said Adam, not taking his eyes off Ruby. 'It has all my important documents in it. I rang your store manager a few moments ago and she said she'd keep hold of it for me. I'd be very grateful if you could fetch it for me. I've a plane to catch.'

'Sure, I'll be right back,' said the woman.

Neither Ruby nor Adam turned to watch her go.

For a long moment, they stared at each other. Ruby had planned exactly what she was going to say during her flight but now that he was in front of her all she wanted to do was fling her arms around his neck and bury her face in his neck. Would he welcome her or had she left it too late?

'I read your book,' she said eventually.

Adam nodded once, waiting for more.

'I only started it yesterday,' she explained.

'I see,' he said.

'And by that I mean I only opened it yesterday evening. For the first time. I hadn't seen your message before that. I mean ... I wanted to say that ... even when you came to the house I was going to ... but I didn't because I was scared.'

'Well, that's very clear,' said Adam, his lovely face breaking into a smile.

He opened his arms and Ruby

stepped into his embrace. Underneath the smell of coffee and city she could sense his unique citrus smell. She was home and suddenly the words were simple.

'I love you,' she said.

Adam laughed, 'I love you too, you crazy lady.'

Adam kissed her hard and fast and she responded fiercely. They broke apart when they sensed someone hovering in the background.

'I've got your bag,' said the store assistant, grinning at them both.

'Thank you very much,' said Adam.

'No problem at all. You both have a nice day now,' the assistant said with a laugh in her voice.

Adam slung an arm around Ruby. 'Thanks, we will,' he said as he tugged Ruby out of the store.

'You've got a flight to catch,' said Ruby, her throat constricting at the thought.

'I have,' said Adam. 'I'm flying to JFK and then I've got a few days in

New York before I return to Britain. I was hoping you'd be free to show me around.'

'You were?' asked Ruby, amazed.

'I was hoping that the reason you'd not responded to my note at all was that you hadn't read it and not that you were repelled by the idea. I should have been braver when I was at your home and told you how I felt about you.'

'I should have told you how I felt. I was planning to all through dinner but I lost my nerve when I realised you were leaving so quickly. It made me think you didn't care for me after all.'

'When you didn't speak to me after the book signing I thought that you didn't care for me either,' said Adam, grinning.

'I was trying to honour our agreement not to speak to each other,' she explained.

'Ah yes, that ridiculous idea. The last nine weeks have been tortuous. Let's agree not to do that again.' Adam tugged her close into his side and Ruby wrapped her arms around his waist. It was getting difficult to walk but she didn't care.

She nestled further into his arms. 'The problem is that we do still live in two different countries.'

'I can write anywhere,' said Adam.

Ruby froze. She stepped away from him. She wanted to look directly at his face. Was he saying what she thought he was saying?

'You would move here?' she asked, not daring to believe that he would do that for her.

Adam grinned. 'Not right here on this street corner, I do need somewhere to plug my computer in. But yes, I could live in Stanmore with you and your family — if you'd let me.'

Ruby yelped in delight and flung both her arms around his waist. She squeezed him hard, not able to believe such a wonderful man would make such a move just for her.

'I would love you to live with me and my family. Grams would be beside herself,' she said.

'Well, if Grams wants me to then it's settled,' said Adam, grinning.

Ruby laughed. '*I* really want you to.'

'Good,' said Adam, cupping her face in his hands and lowering his mouth to hers.

Epilogue: One Year Later

'Do you really need another copy?' Adam asked Ruby.

'But look at how pretty this one is,' insisted Ruby. 'It's got a picture of Melveryn Manor on the front and,' she said, flicking to the middle of Charles Henry's book of poetry, 'a collection of Laura's photographs. Look — there's Pops.'

'So there is,' said Adam, taking the book from her and flicking through it. 'Let's get a couple of copies. Grams would love one of her own.'

Ruby felt her heart clench with love for Adam for thinking of Grams. Over the last year, since Adam had made the move to the States, he'd come to be an important part of her family. Grams was already calling him the grandson she'd never had and the two of them often spent evenings discussing gruesome crime writing together.

To Grams' eternal pride Adam had dedicated his latest novel to her. Grams now carried the book round with her in her handbag and whipped it out to show people at every opportunity.

'Shall we stop for a cup of tea and some cake?' asked Adam.

'I thought that was why we were here,' said Ruby, picking up an extra copy of the book of poetry and adding a Melveryn Manor pen to her pile of purchases.

It was strange to come back to the manor almost a year after they'd left it. In most respects it was still the same grand manor house that they'd left behind, but after the release of Charles' poetry there had been a huge surge in interest in the place. This season the house was open every day to the public and a small shop, with Melveryn Manor merchandise, had been added. Ruby was really enjoying spending time in the shop and on top of her two books of poetry and pen, she was also planning to buy a tea towel and a novelty hat.

When they'd planned their trip to

Britain Adam had suggested that they return to Carwyn Bay for a couple of days to see the changes. Ruby had readily agreed. After a whistle-stop tour of Adam's family and friends, it was good to have a few days to themselves before they headed to Dylan's house for a week's visit.

Ruby had been nervous about meeting Adam's parents; she'd been concerned that they'd be resentful towards her because of Adam's move to the States. She needn't have worried. They'd been warm and welcoming and so happy to see their son content with her. After a restful week with his family they'd travelled to Bristol to stay with Nick and Clara.

Expecting the weekend to be tense, Ruby really hadn't wanted to go but she'd understood that Adam's relationship with Nick was important and so she'd gone along with the trip to support him. They hadn't been at his friend's home for more than an hour when Clara had taken Ruby to one side and hugged her tightly.

'I was so anxious about meeting you,' Clara said, 'but now that I have I'm so pleased that Adam has met someone as lovely as you. I've seen him laugh and smile more in the last sixty minutes than I did in the entire time I knew him. You are so good together.'

After that, the rest of the weekend had gone swimmingly, especially after Clara and Ruby had discovered their shared love of chocolate cake and prosecco. They were perfectly content to sit and chat while the two men talked crime.

Even so, it was good to have some time to themselves now and Ruby was enjoying her trip down memory lane.

Ruby led the way to the coffee shop, stopping at the threshold to savour the familiar sight. The same checked tablecloths and plastic flowers still topped the tables but the room had been extended and more than one worker stood behind the counter taking orders.

'Let's order and see if we can get a seat outside,' suggested Ruby, joining a short queue.

'What are you going to have?' asked Adam as he stood behind her and picked up a menu.

'I'm going to take a look at their cake display and then decide what I fancy.'

'I doubt any of them will be as good as yours,' said Adam with a grin.

'That's true,' said Ruby, grinning as she reached the cabinet. What she saw on the bottom shelf made her pause.

She turned and tugged on Adam's sleeve.

'What is it?' he asked.

'Look at that,' she whispered. 'They've put a sunken lemon drizzle cake on display. Have they gone totally mad?'

Adam took a long look at the cake.

'Excuse me,' he said, catching the attention of a girl serving behind the counter. 'Could you tell me about the cake that looks like a lemon drizzle on the bottom here?'

'That's Sunken Lemon Drizzle,' said the girl.

'I'm sorry,' said Ruby, 'can you say that again?'

'Yes, it's Sunken . . . '

'You mean it's meant to look like that?' asked Ruby incredulously. Beside her she could feel Adam begin to quiver with suppressed laughter.

'Yes, because it's sunken,' explained the waitress patiently.

'Right,' said Ruby slowly. 'In that case may I have a slice? Adam, would you like a piece too?'

'Yes please,' he said, his voice full of the laughter bubbling up inside him.

Adam managed to get out of the café and into a seat before he erupted with laughter.

'How many of those cakes did you make and throw away because they'd sunk in the middle?' he managed to wheeze.

'Thirty-four,' said Ruby.

'Thirty . . . ' but Adam couldn't finish as tears ran down his face. His laughter was infectious and soon Ruby couldn't contain herself either. Other customers glanced round to see what was so funny. Every attempt to get their laughter under control produced fresh gales of laughter.

They managed to contain themselves long enough for Ruby to take a bite and say, 'It tastes just like mine too,' which set Adam off again.

Ruby watched him fondly. She'd been told many times that Adam hadn't smiled much before he'd met her but she couldn't really imagine it. The man she knew smiled and laughed all the time.

Adam wiped his eyes. 'Ruby, you are so funny.'

She grinned at him. This time she hadn't set out to make him laugh but she loved seeing him so happy, so she'd take the compliment. She took another bite of the cake and closed her eyes to savour the tartly sweet flavour.

'Ruby,' said Adam, suddenly serious.

Her eyes snapped open at his sudden change in tone. His expression had changed in the few seconds since she'd last looked at him.

'What's wrong?' she asked, reaching

across the table to touch her fingers to the back of his hand.

'Nothing,' he said, a ghost of a smile chasing across his lips. 'Ruby,' he said again. 'You've made me so happy over the last year.'

She smiled adoringly at him. 'I feel just the same about you,' she said, wondering why he was being so solemn. Today was a happy day.

Adam stood up from his chair and then sank down onto one knee and pulled a small box out of his jacket pocket. He cleared his throat.

'Ruby Turner, will you marry me?'

For a second Ruby could only stare at him. Then she squealed and shouted, 'Yes! Yes. Of course I'll marry you.'

Adam barely had time to slide the engagement ring on her finger before she threw her arms around his neck, knocking him off balance and bringing them both crashing to the floor.

Cheers sounded from the other customers as Adam murmured against her lips, 'I'm looking forward to a lifetime of baking disasters and many, many adventures together.'

Ruby laughed and then kissed him. Life was perfect.

For Ruby's Lemon Drizzle Cake please see recipe on the next page

Lemon Drizzle Cake

Ingredients
125g (4oz) butter
175 g (6oz) caster sugar
2 large eggs
175 g (6oz) self-raising flour
2 lemons, preferably unwaxed
50g (2oz) granulated sugar

1. Preheat the oven to 180°C, gas mark 4. Lightly oil and line the base of an 18cm (7in) tin with baking paper.
2. In a large bowl, cream the butter and sugar together until soft and fluffy. In a separate bowl beat the eggs together. Gradually add a little of the egg to the creamed mixture adding 1tbsp flour after each addition.
3. Take one of the lemons and finely grate the rind. Stir into the creamed mixture until smooth and then add the juice of the lemon into the mixture.

Pour into the tin and bake for 25–30 minutes.

For the topping

1. Zest the remaining lemon, mix it with 25g (1oz) granulated sugar and set aside. Squeeze out the juice out of the last lemon and put it into a small saucepan and add the remaining granulated sugar. Gently heat the mixture, stirring it occasionally. When the sugar has dissolved, simmer gently until it turns syrupy (2–4min).

2. Once the cake has been removed from the oven prick it all over the top. Sprinkle the lemon zest and sugar over the top of the cake and finally drizzle over the syrup.

We do hope that you have enjoyed reading this large print book.

Did you know that all of our titles are available for purchase?

We publish a wide range of high quality large print books including:
Romances, Mysteries, Classics
General Fiction
Non Fiction and Westerns

Special interest titles available in large print are:
The Little Oxford Dictionary
Music Book, Song Book
Hymn Book, Service Book

Also available from us courtesy of Oxford University Press:
Young Readers' Dictionary
(large print edition)
Young Readers' Thesaurus
(large print edition)

For further information or a free brochure, please contact us at:
Ulverscroft Large Print Books Ltd.,
The Green, Bradgate Road, Anstey,
Leicester, LE7 7FU, England.
Tel: (00 44) **0116 236 4325**
Fax: (00 44) **0116 234 0205**

THE LOCKET OF
LOGAN HALL

Christina Garbutt

Newly widowed Emily believes she
will never love again. Working as an
assistant in flirtatious Cameron's
antiques shop, she finds a romantic
keepsake in an old writing desk.
Emily and Cameron set off on a
hunt for the original owner, and the
discoveries they make on the way
change both of them forever. But
Emily doesn't realise that Cameron
is slowly falling in love with her. Is
his love doomed to be unrequited,
or will Emily see what's right in
front of her — before it's too late?

PARADISE FOUND

Sarah Purdue

Carrie's first visit to Chatterham House, where her grandparents lived and worked, becomes an unexpected turning point in her life when her relationship with her boyfriend ends disastrously there; but she meets Edward, a handsome employee who shares her interest in the estate's history. When she begins volunteering at the house on weekends, she feels drawn to Edward — but the icily beautiful Portia seems to have a claim on him, and his only explanation is that it's 'complicated'. Will Carrie decide he's worth risking her heart for?

A MERRY BRAMBLEWICK CHRISTMAS

Sharon Booth

Recovering from a break-up, Izzy is throwing herself into the primary school Christmas play — it's a huge project, even with fellow teacher and volunteer assistant Ash by her side. As Christmas draws nearer and the snow begins to fall, Izzy and Ash develop a warm and growing attraction. But Izzy's best friend Anna has been acting coldly towards her since she revealed the reason her last relationship ended. With Anna judging her so harshly, dare Izzy tell Ash the truth about herself and risk everything they have built so far?

KINDRED HEARTS

Wendy Kremer

After a humiliating break-up, Kate decides to spend Christmas alone in a secluded countryside cottage. But her plans for solitude evaporate when she meets the guest at the neighbouring cottage — exciting, unpredictable Alex. As Kate continues to bump into Alex in unexpected places, her oldest and best friend Chris warns her off her new acquaintance. She is furious — who is he to interfere? But as she realises that Alex might not be what she is searching for, Kate wonders if she's been looking for love in all the wrong places . . .

A CHRISTMAS BETROTHAL

Fenella J. Miller

Obliged to seek shelter from the storm, Lord Ralph Didsbury diverts to a nearby house, closely followed by Lady Winterton and her two grand-daughters, Persephone and Aphrodite. But the house appears unoccupied, and when two further travel-weary gentlemen join the party, there is still no sign of the owner. Why is he hiding away? And are these young gentlemen who they purport to be? Ralph intends to find out, but as the appalling weather intensifies, so do his feelings for Persephone, and it is proving to be quite a distraction . . .

THE HOLIDAY DOCTOR

Jane Lester

After a hiatus of four years, Susan Vengrove returns with her family to their beloved holiday destination of Holland Green. But the village has changed — as has Dr. Gerald Adams, known to them as the 'Holiday Doctor'. Every villager appears to be hiding a secret, and Dr. Adams seems more distant, leading Susan to wonder if it's the passage of time or the fact that she's now eighteen. However, just as she begins to recognise her growing romantic feelings for the doctor, his own secret surfaces — he has a fiancée . . .